I0571607

THE ZOMBIES
OF MESMER

A NICKIE NICK VAMPIRE HUNTER NOVEL

THE ZOMBIES
OF MESMER

A NICKIE NICK VAMPIRE HUNTER NOVEL

by O. M. Grey

BLUE MOOSE PRESS

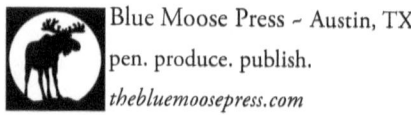 Blue Moose Press ~ Austin, TX
pen. produce. publish.
thebluemoosepress.com

ISBN-13: 978-1-936960-92-7
First Edition. Second Printing.

ATTENTION ORGANIZATIONS AND SCHOOLS:
Quantity discounts are available on bulk purchases of this book for educational purposes or fund raising.

For more information, go to
thebluemoosepress.com
omgrey.wordpress.com

Library of Congress Control Number: 2011961321
Grey, O. M., 1969 -
    Avalon Revisited / by O. M. Grey
1. Paranormal Romance--Fiction. II. Title.
ISBN-13: 978-1-936960-92-7

Printed in the United States of America

In Loving Memory of Cherished Doghters

Bronte, Star & Oreo

You are sorely missed, my sweet girls.
My heart breaks again every day without you.

CHAPTER ONE

IN WHICH NICKIE NICK
DISCOVERS HER DESTINY

The toes of my oversized boots searched for footing along the back of the countertop as I slid through the small back window, clutching the sill for support. I always came in and out of the pantry window when I went on my "adventures," as Fanny the Nanny called them. My parents would never dare come into this part of the house. It simply was not done, as it only held the laundry room, pantry, and kitchen. It was a place for servants, and my parents would not lower themselves enough to be in a place of servitude. The servants themselves were not down here unless it was just before or just after a meal. So even if they caught me, they would not tell my parents. Not even Fanny would tell.

I lowered myself to a standing position and brushed the snow from my patched overcoat, dusting the sink with a sprinkling of snowflakes which melted almost as soon as they hit the countertop. A sudden, insistent clacking sound startled me. I turned from the window to see Fanny glaring up at me and impatiently tapping her pointed black boot against the pantry's stone floor.

"Where have you been?" Fanny the Nanny scolded. She was not really my nanny, of course. No seventeen-year-old girl needed a nanny. She was more like a governess, but I still liked the sound of Fanny the Nanny. And more importantly, she didn't.

"Out," I replied in mock defiance, crossing my arms and holding my ground.

"Just look at you. You are a mess, and you must make your grand entrance within the hour! The party is about to begin and your guests will be arriving any minute." She stood glaring up at me with her chubby hands balled up in fists and set firmly on her hips. "Get down from there this instant, young lady. What would your mother say?"

"She would not say a thing, Fanny, because you shall not tell her a thing," I replied, taking her proffered hand and jumping down onto the stone floor beside her.

"You have been with that Conrad again, haven't you?"

"Not just Conrad. With Franklin, Rufus, and Edwin as well," I replied with a smirk, which would have sounded so scandalous to any passersby, a girl talking about all the boys with whom she had been keeping company. But it was far from scandalous. "They are just friends, Fanny, as you well know." But she did like to tease nonetheless.

"Friends or no, my lamb. You are cutting it very close tonight."

I took off my scarf and cap, letting my dark hair fall about my shoulders, still damp from the quickly melting snowflakes. With the gas range in the adjacent kitchen, burning virtually all day and night, it was rather hot on this level. Quite the change from the bitter sting of the London's streets in December. "They were cold and hungry, and I was not going to leave them out there like that. Birthday or not."

Fanny flashed me a smile, then sighed, "Always thinking of others. Tenderhearted, you are." She took my hat and scarf, then held out her hand again waiting for my overcoat. I unbuttoned it and handed it over, revealing a dingy waistcoat over a pair of dirty dungarees. "Ugh," Fanny grunted. "Upstairs with you, young lady. Wash up and get out of those awful clothes. I never should have gotten them for you."

"Just think how much worse it would be if I had gone in my fine white dress?" I teased, then spun around the pantry as if dancing at a ball.

Fanny laughed and shook her head. I loved making her laugh with my antics, as long as mother was not around. With mother, it was all propriety and tedium. With Fanny, I could be myself.

"Boots, too." She pointed to the filthy, wet boots on my feet and the muddy footprints marking the steps of my mock waltz.

"Oops." I eased them off, smearing more packed, muddy snow on the stone floor. I gave Fanny my best *please-forgive-me* expression and batted my eyelashes once or twice.

"Upstairs with you, missy," she scolded and flicked the scarf at my derrière as I left. "Don't you dare let your mother see you like that. I should never hear the end of it," she called after me.

To be safe, I used the servant's back staircase to get upstairs, and after checking that my parents were nowhere in sight, I snuck across the hardwood floors in my stocking feet on tip toes, careful not to slip. I made my way down the hall and disappeared into my bedchamber, undetected. Just as I was closing my chamber door, the music for my impending debutante ball floated up the main staircase and filled me with dread.

"We must do what society demands," I said aloud in a mocking sing-song way, repeating what my mother said to me far too often.

I shall play their game and draw out this marriage thing as long as I can, hopefully until I will be regarded a spinster. Then I can get on with more interesting pursuits in life, like learning and traveling.

I dreamt of going on the Grand Tour and helping people who were not as fortunate or "well-born," whatever that meant.

I shuddered when I saw the fine white ball gown with its frills and ruffles and short lacy sleeves spread out on my bed. A pair of white gloves lay across the dress, and all I wanted to do was to smear the dirt from my hands all over them. How I loathed this day.

The water in the corner wash basin was still lukewarm. After removing my dingy boy's clothes, I stood before the small mirror in just my camisole and pantalettes and, regarding myself, took a deep breath to stop the tears from coming. I took the white washcloth and washed my face, hands, and arms. At least I got the satisfaction of staining their ceremonial white washcloth. When I was finished with it, it was as dingy as the boy's clothes in which I felt so much more comfortable. I picked up the brush and began to brush my hair. It was naturally curly, which would be a blessing this evening, as there was no time to curl it before my grand entrance.

Mother insisted on me making a grand entrance, American style.

Traditionally, the debutante was to greet all her guests as they arrived, but mother wanted to do it the new way. She was a paradox, both ashamed of being considered of the *nouveau riche*, fairly new into London's society, and at the same time trumpeting her American heritage and modern ways.

I heard the door close behind me, and I turned to see Fanny enter frantically. She held a steaming pot of water. "Still not finished washing up?" she said in her strong Scottish brogue.

She rushed over, put the kettle on an iron trivet next to the wooden washbasin stand, and then, with a look of disgust back at me, took the cloudy water over to my bedroom window. When she opened it, a gust of refreshingly cold wind blew in, carrying a few stray snowflakes, and it filled my heart with momentary joy. Brisk, beautiful winter weather.

Fanny tossed the dirty water out the window into the alley below before shutting and locking the window, along with my joy, bringing me back to the reality at hand.

"Perhaps we can make some excuse, like I'm deathly ill. Then I shan't have to parade around like a peacock, on display for all the eligible bachelors. It is like I'm nothing more than chattle or a sheep on market days, presented for the picking."

"Now, Nickie, we have discussed this. It is just one night. You can make due for just one night." Steam rose toward the ceiling as she poured the fresh water into the now empty basin. Taking the browned washcloth between the utmost tip of her thumb and forefinger (with another sneer of exaggerated disgust), she dipped it into the hot water and started scrubbing places I had obviously missed.

"Balderdash, one night. They are trying to plan the rest of my life! I'm most certainly no debutante, and I have absolutely no interest in marriage at seventeen. I just want to be left alone, and I really hate white, frilly dresses." I pouted and crossed my arms like a petulant child.

"We must get you into that frilly white dress and fix this rats' nest." She turned a blind eye to my mock tantrum, trading the washcloth for the hairbrush and tugging against the tangles.

I bit my lip and tried not to cry out. It felt as if she would pull the hair from my head.

"One should enjoy their seventeenth birthday, shouldn't one? But not me, no sir."

"Quickly," she said, ignoring my continued protests and putting the brush on the washbasin stand's lower shelf. "Corset."

There was that feeling of dread again. Corsets. Not fun. I assumed the position. Against the corner of my four poster bed, I hugged one of the ornately turned shafts and waited as Fanny laced the back of the corset over my camisole and pantalettes.

"Do you think they will find a husband for me tonight," I asked Fanny quietly.

"Possibly. There were already many guests arriving as I headed upstairs. We really must hurry."

"I don't wish to marry for duty. I want to marry for love."

"Yes. You and every other girl in your position. Such is life in these times. At your station," she replied matter-of-factly.

"Then I don't wish to marry at all."

"I'm afraid that's not up to me, nor is it really up to you, if you want to gain your inheritance," Fanny said with a hint of sadness in her voice.

"The devil with my inheritance. They can send me into the country—or off as a governess or even put me to work in their blasted factory dying linen, but I shall never submit to marry. After all, you never married."

"It is just one night," she reminded me again.

"Of course, what society demands," I sneered. "The ball is one thing, and I suppose it will be relatively painless, but I absolutely will not submit to marry someone I don't fancy."

She tugged on the strings of the corset and cinched it snugly around my middle. I caught my breath and tried to push the front of it down beneath my breasts.

"Leave it alone." Fanny swatted my hand away. "Relax your breath or I will not be able to close it."

"I shan't be able to breathe," I protested.

"You will not have to breathe, much. You'll just be standing around and dancing some, not the level of activity you are used to, my dear," she said with a hint of sarcasm, referring to my adventures. "I'm quite sure you will be just fine." She wrenched the corset tighter, causing me to grasp the bed post more firmly to avoid being pulled away from it. "Have you been sneaking apple tarts again?" she asked with an accusatory lilt. "This is rather difficult to close tonight, my lamb. Hold on tight."

I couldn't take a deep breath as the corset already confined me too much for that, so I took a shallow breath and held onto the bedpost more tightly than ever.

A chill ran up my back, and I looked over at the window thinking another gust of the winter air had come through, but it was still closed tightly. The chill continued and filled my entire body. I watched the goose bumps travel up my bare arms. Then the chill turned to a burning fire that surged through my limbs, chasing the goose bumps away. Colors became brighter around me. The scent of new satin filled my nostrils and I heard guests milling about downstairs through my closed door. My entire body felt full of energy. Life. Strength. Power.

"One, two...three," Fanny counted. As she reached "three," she pulled with all her might and I held on to the bedpost with all mine. With a loud crack, I fell backwards onto Fanny with the bedpost still in my arms!

"Oh, my graces!" Fanny exclaimed.

"I–I'm sorry," I stammered, pushing the broken bedpost away from us. "I didn't mean to, Fanny. It just came off in my arms!" Moving off Fanny, I looked up at the bed trying to make sense of what just happened. The canopy sagged on the corner onto which I was so recently holding. The other three posts still held up the wooden frame around the top from falling completely, but it definitely sagged.

"Oh, my graces!" Fanny said again. "It has happened. Hasn't it?"

"What?" I was still not sure how I broke the thick post off from the rest of the bed. I turned back to Fanny on the floor with me. She looked at me with an open mouth and wide eyes, as if I was some sort of circus sideshow exhibition.

"The prophecy! You are she after all," she said, eyes wide. Her trembling hands covered her cheeks. "I thought when nothing happened today that the witches had been mistaken, but you are her after all!" Fanny exclaimed again. She sat on the floor staring up at me in surprise and her skirts crumpled beneath her.

"What witches? What are you talking about?" I demanded.

A knock at the door interrupted us.

"Nicole?" My mother's voice sounded muffled through the door, but her tone made it quite clear that she was rather impatient. "It is almost time. I do hope you are dressed."

"Just a moment!" Fanny's shrill, excited voice filled the room. "We shall be down presently, madam. Don't look! We want you to be surprised at your own daughter's beauty. Oh, and she does look lovely, madam. So very lovely." Fanny took the broken post and shoved it under the bed. "We'll be down presently," she repeated.

"Very well, but do make haste," my mother said through the door. Her footsteps trailed down the hallway and I let out the breath I didn't know I had been holding.

Fanny sighed a relief next to me.

"Quickly." Fanny scrambled to her feet. "I must get this corset fastened and you in that dress. Hold still," she said, jerking me up and grabbing hold of the corset strings again.

"What witches!" I demanded.

She cinched the corset as tight as she could.

"Let us hope we can fasten your dress, or you will be quite the sight," she said, ignoring my question. She was ignoring a lot of my comments tonight. "I cannot cinch this corset closed. You and those apple tarts!"

After I felt her tie the corset off at the bottom, I spun around and took her by the shoulders. "What witches, Fanny? What prophecy? What just happened?"

"There is not time for it now." She pulled herself from my grasp and gathered the white dress from the bed. "Put on your petticoat. There is no time for dawdling!"

"I will not do another thing until you answer my questions," I insisted, placing my fists firmly on my hips.

She sighed, defeated. "Very well. Put on the petticoat, and I shall tell you as you dress." She stuck a chubby finger in my face. "But you must promise me that nothing I say will stop you from behaving properly tonight at your ball. It is very important, now more than ever, that you keep up appearances. Do you understand me?" She turned and gathered up the frilly dress from the bed.

"That depends on what you say, Fanny. You are frightening me." Chills ran up my arms. I tried to warm them away by rubbing my hands over my bare skin, but nothing could take the feeling away. Something had changed in that moment. I had changed.

"Promise me, Nicole." She stood there with the white dress in her hands and looked at me with a very serious expression. I had never in all my life seen her look so dour, yet at the same time, I did see a hint of joy in her eyes.

"All right," I gave in. "I promise. Now tell me." I stepped into the petticoat and tied it around my back. She put the white dress over my head and arms, and while my head was still covered by the white satin she said, "Your birth fulfilled an age-old prophecy that a Hawthorne would be born prematurely on Midwinter's Night, and on the seventeenth year from the day of her birth, she would be called upon and bestowed with the powers necessary to protect humanity from evil supernatural fiends like vampires."

My head cleared the white satin and I looked at Fanny the Nanny, expecting to see some sign that she was just having me on, but there was none.

"Evil supernatural fiends? Vampires? Really, Fanny. Is this all a game?"

"No, my dear. I should have told you before tonight, but there had been no signs before, well," she said with a look back to the broken bed.

"This is preposterous!" But there was no denying the change I had felt run through me. Something was definitely different. Still, evil supernatural fiends? Please.

She hurriedly fastened my dress in the back and fluffed up the blasted bustle. I truly did hate those frivolous things. Leading me to the dressing table, she pushed me down in the chair and began working on my hair.

"Quickly now, the powder and blush. We shall have to work together. Your mother will no doubt be coming back soon to collect you."

"You *are* serious." The look on her face made that clear. I picked up the powder puff and tended to the shine on my nose, cheeks, and shoulders. The white gown had a rather wide décolletage, so there was much skin to cover.

Fanny swept my chestnut curls up into a loose twist and fastened it with a silver hair comb.

"I'm quite serious, my dear. Oh my, I just really don't know where to begin, and we have so little time," she said while twisting a few stray locks into place along the side of my face. I began putting some color on my cheeks and lips.

"How about the beginning?" I offered. I was doing my best to remain calm, and the tight corset certainly reminded me not to get overly excited and remain quite proper and still. Society dictates that ladies must keep their feelings well hidden. After living in this household for so many years, I excelled in skills that would be essential to make it through this night. Especially now.

"I come from a long line of witches, and we have watched your family for generations. It was your ancestor John Hathorne who condemned some of the witches in Salem over in The Colonies. After that, the American coven wrote to their sister coven here in the England about a series of dreams they had had after those horrid trials were over. They dreamed that a descendant of Hathorne would one day set it right. It would be a girl and she would inherit the powers of the damned to be used for good, working with the witches and fighting the vampires, demons, and even fey from the unseelie court."

"Vampires?" I said with a derisive scoff. "Really?"

"Listen child," she began as she draped a string of pearls around my neck and fastened them in the back. "This is no jest. You wanted to hear it before your ball, so I'm telling you quickly. We can talk in more detail later."

"All right." I found all this rather hard to believe. It was merely another of Fanny's strange stories, just as she had told me my whole life. She was just telling me another ghost story to entertain me before the ball. That's all this was.

"You were conceived on Beltane, a holy day for my people and the day associated with the holy hawthorn tree, from which your family were originally named. You were born on a moor a mere seven and a half months later, premature, on Midwinter's Night. It was exactly where my coven had foretold: The Forest of Bowland in Yorkshire."

"A moor in Yorkshire. Really?" I said, still not believing her. "What a tale you tell."

She pinned a few curls into place and decorated them with some fripperies as I clipped the pearl earrings onto my earlobes. "Yes. A moor. Your parents were resting in the country during the latter part of the pregnancy, but your father got word from the factory that needed to be dealt with presently."

"Of course," I breathed through clenched teeth. That I believed. "Business always comes first." It was why I hardly knew my parents. I had always been second to their precious textile factory.

"Your boots." She knelt beside me, and I offered her my stockinged feet. She went to work lacing them up and continued, "Your mother didn't want to be left behind, insisting that there was much time before the due date. Although her doctors advised her against it, they left early morning on the 21st, dreaming of Christmas in the city, but the driver took a wrong turn which ended in tragedy for him and almost for you and your mother. After hitting a large stone on the moor, it set your mother into labor. I was nearby, and not by accident, as it was where your birth had been foretold, as I previously said. Since I was a trained midwife, I delivered you. You were so very tiny. Three fortnights early, you were. It is a miracle you survived, especially after such a traumatic birth on such a bitterly cold night."

She straightened my skirts over the white boots, got up from her kneeling position, and started fussing with my hair again. "I held you in my arms and I felt the definition of love. I understood the purpose of life. You were powerful even then, Nick."

She reached around the back of her neck to unclasp a necklace and then lifted it out of the front of her bodice. Offering it to me, she said, "This is a powerful amulet, my dove. It will protect you from a vampire's mind power. They will be unable to compel you or influence your thoughts. Keep a clear head, my lamb."

"Thank you, Fanny." I allowed her to clasp the necklace around my own neck. The large black stone cradled in silver hung from a heavy chain.

"You may tuck it inside your gown, for I know it is old and rather garish."

"Nonsense. 'Tis beautiful, and I shall cherish it always. Although I will normally keep it protected, close to my heart, tonight I shall display it proudly for all to see."

Tears filled her eyes and her nose turned red. I looked at her reflection through my dressing table mirror, and I knew this was all the truth. I felt it, just as I felt the power of which she spoke surging through me. I wanted to scream. To run. To fly, but I had to sit with my hands folded properly in my lap. I had to go downstairs and dance with potential husbands. I had to—

Another knock, more frantic than the last interrupted my thoughts.

"Nicole!" my mother demanded. "Your guests are waiting!"

"Coming mother." I got up and turned to Fanny. The tears spilled down her plump cheeks and she looked at me with love. I went in to embrace her, but she stopped me.

"No, you will smudge your powder. Remember what I said, act properly tonight, but have a nice time. One only turns seventeen once. We shall talk more later."

"We most certainly shall!" I said in a scolding tone, but with a smile in my voice and on my face. She smiled back at me and wiped the tears from her rosy cheeks.

"Don't forget your gloves." She indicated the long white gloves still on the bed.

I collected them and put them on hurriedly as I turned to leave, but she stopped me with a single word.

"Nicole."

I turned back to her with my gloved hand resting on the door handle, my mother still pounding on the other side of the door.

"It was I who suggested you be named Nicole. Unusual name for this part of the world, I know, but it means 'Victory of the People.' And of that I have no doubt, my dear girl." She wiped more tears from her cheeks.

Willing my own tears away, I turned the door handle to face my determined mother, but it broke off in my hand. I looked back at Fanny for guidance.

"Take care tonight," she added, laughing now. "You are stronger than you think."

Chapter Two

In Which Nickie Nick Dances by Rote

Upturned, expectant faces filled the room below as I stood at the top of the staircase unable to move. The muscles in my cheeks complained as I held a plastered smile on my face. My gloved hand rested delicately on the wooden banister, but my mind was still back in my bedchamber.

Me? Really?

I was supposed to fight vampires? *And* demons?

Had I heard that right?

Surely Fanny was joking, or maybe she just had had too much whiskey.

"May I present," a loud booming voice filled the room, "Miss Nicole Knickerbocker Hawthorn."

Fanny did enjoy a taste every now and again, but the strength and, for lack of a better word, *power* surging through me was no mistake. It was no joke. Something was quite different indeed.

"Nicole," my mother chided in a harsh whisper through her own plastered smile. She was standing a few feet away from me on the second story. "Nicole. Move!"

This jolted me out of my thoughts. The music had already started again, which was my cue, so I began my slow descent of the staircase. Mother had made me practice this several times a day over the past week, so I knew just how slowly to move and just how wide to smile. I really had hated all those stupid rehearsals at the time. I mean, I could walk down a staircase and smile without practice. Now, however, I was truly grateful that my body could do this all without my brain being in gear. Because my mind certainly was not operating properly at the moment.

As I reached the bottom of the staircase, the guests gathered around to greet me as I made my way through the foyer. My mother was right behind me with her hand at the small of my back, guiding me.

Again. Grateful.

A rather large, old, and particularly pasty woman stopped us on our way to the dining hall which had been converted into a ballroom for the party.

"So lovely," she said, then added to my mother, "You must be very proud."

"I am, indeed," my mother answered. I could feel the joy emanating off of her in a warm glowy way. At least she was enjoying this. My face was beginning to ache from keeping the same smile for so long. The corner of my mouth started to twitch.

"Nicole." The pasty woman gave one of those condescending smiles. "Such an unusual name."

"Yes," I offered, my cheek muscles welcoming the momentary rest. "It is Greek. It means—"

"Foolish girl," my mother interrupted as she moved up beside me and grabbed my arm. I noticed a blush coming up in her cheeks. "It is a family name, actually. Dutch. She is named after my family, from the Nicoles and Knickerbockers of Holland, and more recently, New York."

"I see," the woman said, clenching her teeth. "Still, so lovely. Yes, so very lovely."

My mother's grip clamped down on my gloved arm, for the gloves extended well past my elbows, nearly to the bottom of the tiny dress sleeves. Mother steered me back on course toward the far end of the ballroom floor. There we stopped and the guests formed a receiving line, each to meet me formally as I entered society.

The entire thing seemed so pointless, really.

They greeted my mother first and then she presented me to each of them saying, "I want to present my daughter, Nicole" to every. single. one. of them.

I smiled. I greeted. I curtsied. I did all that was expected of me.

After an eternity of pretense, the receiving line was finally coming to an end. There had been more than a few handsome bachelors, and even more old crotchety ones, who took great pleasure in kissing my gloved hand and reserving their place on my dance card. Not one of them piqued my interest. Not even the handsome ones. After all, I did have more important things to think about than with whom to dance and when. How perfectly frivolous.

But dance I must.

The first came for his dance, and I waltzed with him just as I was taught. I really couldn't say what we talked about. Something trivial, no doubt, as I was able to carry on the conversation without my thoughts ever leaving what Fanny had said. There was a great difference between who *the ton* saw and who I really was on the inside. Fanny had taught me to blend into High Society quite well.

Vampires. What were they like? Could they be here at my ball? And demons! How dreadfully horrifying!

And this was the way I spent the evening, waltz after waltz. Each with a new dance partner that hardly registered in my distracted mind until...

"You are not listening to a word I say, are you Miss Hawthorn?" my current partner accused. I looked up at him and saw it was none other than the great fop, His Most Annoying, Lord Reginald Godwyn. He was considered one of the most eligible bachelors for one of my station, that's the half-American daughter of *nouveau riche* industrialists. Only those titled with questionable finances would lower themselves enough to marry beneath them, or what would have been considered beneath them only a few years ago. The upper middle-class was now marrying quite often into the lower aristocracy.

"I beg your pardon, sir?" I feigned offense.

"I said, you are not listening to anything I'm saying, are you?" he repeated as he twirled me in a waltz across the ballroom. Waltzing was second nature to me, almost like walking. I was normally able to do it quite well without thinking, but now I found myself counting 'one-two-three, one-two-three' in my head to ensure I would not miss a step.

His Most Annoying had certainly done what he did best. Yet, this irksome, albeit handsome, man was my mother's first choice for my husband. He was the highest rank in attendance, and he must think this is all quite beneath him. We did have that in common.

My daydreaming must have offended him quite deeply. Good. For I would never marry such a man. Best that he lost interest altogether.

"I think one would do one the honor of at least listening when one speaks, wouldn't one?"

"What?" I asked before I could stop myself. Did he really just say that?

"Am I not interesting enough to hold your attention, *Miss* Hawthorn?" He emphasized the 'miss' to indicate that I was neither married nor titled, a subtle way of chastising me. If I had cared about such things, I'm sure it would have stung.

I wanted to say, 'of course not,' but I minded my manners. "Forgive my rudeness, Lord Godwyn. My mind did wander for a moment. Please, do repeat your comment, my lord. You now have my undivided attention."

"It was a question, actually. I shall repeat it dear lady, but you must make more of an effort to listen. Don't you agree?" He was quite handsome, but really in the most obvious and tiresome way. The type of handsome that's too handsome, especially for one as spoiled and elitist as this great fop. And he was indeed a Great Fop! He had perfect blue eyes, a perfect chiseled jaw that framed a brilliant white smile, and perfect color of flaxen hair swept perfectly to the side. Each step he made in the waltz was perfect as well. He was the epitome of what society considered a great catch for any debutante, especially for one at my station, as I was so very often reminded. I would be considered most fortunate to marry such a man, a mere five years my senior. But his beauty was marred by his personality, which was bossy, arrogant, and terribly vexing.

"Yes. Of course, Lord Godwyn. Again, do forgive my rudeness."

"Very well. I am in the market for a wife, if I may be so bold. Perhaps my boldness will hold your attention this time. And I would very much like to call on you on Christmas Day. May I do so, Miss Hawthorn?" Before I could respond he continued. "If all goes well at that meeting, then I would very much like to escort you to a New Year's Ball the following week."

I couldn't understand why he had needed my attention so desperately, as he seemed to have decided this for himself without my acknowledgment.

"Christmas is traditionally a day for family in our home, Lord Godwyn," I said sweetly.

"I have already spoken with your mother, and she has agreed to the visit."

The music had just stopped, so we stood before each other for a moment before he bowed and kissed my white-gloved hand.

"Well, then." I gave him the same sweet smile, "I shall see you in a few days, Lord Godwyn."

"I look forward to it, Miss Hawthorn. You do look quite lovely this evening, despite that repulsive necklace."

I curtsied, and he strutted away.

Over the rest of the evening, I caught Lord Godwyn watching me quite often, and it was deeply unsettling. I glanced over at the great Grandfather Clock in the foyer, counting the minutes to when this disagreeable ball would come to an end and I could get out of this blasted corset and learn more about who I had become, but there was still at least another hour before I could be free. Looking down from the great clock, my eyes met those of a young man who I had never seen before, peering in the long window that ran down the side of the front door. For that instant our eyes locked, my stomach flipped inside my tightly strung corset. He was beautiful, albeit rather scruffy. His face was dirty, but his dark eyes sent a thrill through me like I have never known. But before I could move toward the door, he was gone. From that point on, that mysterious stranger fought the thoughts of my strange birthright for control of my mind.

After the last guest left, I gladly went back up to my chamber and immediately took off that frivolous dress and had begun to unlace my corset when Fanny came in from her adjoining room.

"Did you have a nice time?" she asked cheekily.

"Very funny," I replied. "I'm just so happy it is over."

"Did you find a husband?" She enjoyed playing with me.

My thoughts fled to that handsome stranger in the window, but that was just absurd, as I had no idea who that was and I would likely never see him again. But that feeling is what I wanted in a husband. That rush of thrill and excitement. Whoever he was, I knew now that that feeling was possible. Now more than ever I knew I would not settle for anything less than love.

"Well?" Fanny raised her eyebrows awaiting an answer.

"There were many handsome suitors in attendance, Fanny. Indeed! But, alas, no one at the party stirred any feelings of love for me." It was not a lie after all. That mysterious man had not been at the party.

"So then, we can enjoy each other's company for a while longer."

Fanny was far more like a mother to me than my own, and I knew I was very much like a daughter to her.

She helped me on with my night dress, and I climbed up on my bed and snuggled under the covers. Fanny sat next to me and stoked my hair like she had done my entire life.

"Tell me more about this prophecy, Fanny."

"Very well, you did hold up your end of our agreement. It is known as The Hawthorn Legacy, and it was foretold many, many years before you were born."

"How is that even possible? How can anyone know what will come to pass?"

"My coven is descended from a long line of very powerful witches."

"Are you a witch, too?" I sat up straight against my headboard, waiting for one of her stories. I now began to wonder if all those stories she had told me throughout my life had been real and not just bedtime stories.

"I am," she answered. Her eyes looked sad. "Once, I was a very powerful witch, and I suppose I still am. But I gave up that life to care for you, my lamb. I have kept up a moderate practice, of course, as I have been preparing for this day my entire life. But many members of my coven have grown into extremely powerful forces against darkness."

"So I'm not the only vampire hunter?"

"Heavens, no, child. How could there be only one vampire hunter? This world would be overrun with demons and vampires and other nasties if only one person in the entire world could defeat them. There are many fighting in the war against evil, child; but you are special. You are also The Protector, and you are the only one. No, there have been others, and there will be more once you are...finished. Although, there has not been a Protector like you for generations. Not since your birth was foretold, and your powers do exceed that of most. At least, they were foretold as such. Your actual abilities are yet to be seen. Tell me, did you feel a change?"

I pulled my knees to my chest and looked up at the broken canopy. The corner post I had broken during the change was still missing, but the canopy had been temporarily propped up with a broom handle and some twine.

"Sorry about that." I indicated the broken bed frame.

"No worries, love. Wilfred fixed it for the time being. We shall get it properly tended to tomorrow."

"I guess it goes without saying that I felt a change." Resting my chin on my knees, I thought about the feeling that I had when the change came over me. It was not unlike the feeling in my stomach when I had seen that beautiful stranger, only much more pronounced. Also, it ran through my entire body. "At first it was a chill, then it turned to fire, as if my skin was burning."

"Interesting. Perhaps part of the witches blessing on your family. That was the fate of many a witch, burned at the stake. Such a horrible way to die, my dear. Your Hathorne ancestor ensured women accused of witchcraft met similar ends. Hanged and crushed they were. So horrible. So very horrible, indeed."

"It didn't hurt, Fanny. Rather it was exhilarating, like every pore exploded with strength and energy all at the same time. Then I could see more clearly, if that makes sense. And I could hear things from far away and smell...like all my senses were heightened."

"You are indeed The Protector, my dear. You are the most powerful vampire hunter alive."

"What about you, Fanny. Did you ever hunt vampires and demons?"

"Oh that was many years ago, my dove. Many, many years. I must've been no older than you, but yes, I have dusted a vampire or two in my time. Come here." She got up from the bed and waddled a few steps before she walked the kinks out of her "old bones," as she called them. She led me into her own bedchamber, pulled the rug aside, and opened up a hinged portion of the floorboards.

"This is my past, but it is your future."

Beneath the floor door were dozens of sharpened wood stakes and other weapons.

"We will begin training tomorrow after you have had a chance to rest from this evening's excitement. It is much to take in all at once, no?

She handed me a wooden stake, and it belonged in my hands. I made a fist around the hard shaft and felt the roughness of the wood dimple my skin.

"It is made out of hawthorn wood, the tree from which your ancestors were originally named. This, my dear, is your main weapon for hunting vampires. From this point forward you are to always have a stake on your person."

"Where did you get all these?"

"Some are from my own fighting days, but most I have carved throughout the years in preparation for this day."

She took the black stone that hung around my neck and slid it inside my nightgown. "Keep the necklace tucked close to your breast for protection. It is more powerful when it lies against your skin."

I fingered the stone through the cotton nightdress. "So vampires cannot control my thoughts with this, correct?"

"True."

"But they normally can? I mean, how? Will I be able to do that?"

"So many questions!" Fanny laughed.

"Sorry, Fanny, but this is all rather shocking."

"Yes, they normally can. I'm not sure how, but they can cloud your mind. They can feed off you and make you not remember anything about it. They can make you believe and do things, too. And, no, as far as I know, you will not have that ability."

"But you said–"

"I know I said you would have powers like them, and you will. You do," she corrected herself. "You have strength and speed that rival theirs, but you are still human after all."

"Do they look human?"

"More or less, but they have a tendency to look increasingly less human and more monstrous as time goes on. Really old vampires are quite monstrous, but they can make you believe they are still beautiful. That necklace will keep you from being fooled by that. Their cold, pale flesh and pointy canine teeth normally keep them out of polite company," she assured me, but I was not convinced.

"I saw some rather pale and monstrous looking, lecherous old men at my birthday gala earlier." The memory of some of those suitors caused my lip to curl in the most unattractive way.

Fanny laughed heartily and then covered her mouth. She looked around guiltily as if she could wake my parents across this huge house.

"How will I recognize them?" I asked.

"You will most certainly know one when you seen one," she had responded. That was of little help.

"How? Do they have fangs?"

"Indeed they do."

"Are they always out or do they sometimes look like normal teeth?"

"They are always visible, my dear. Now it is getting late and you need your rest. We have much to do tomorrow."

"Do they come out during the day?"

"They can, but they are out mostly at night because the sun burns and blisters their skin if in it for too long. Also, their strength and powers of mind control weaken during daylight hours. It is why they have what are called powers of darkness."

"But how will I know when I see one?"

She laughed again. "So many questions! With some practice and concentration," she said, "you will be able to sense them. Here." She put her clenched fist against my stomach. "That, along with fighting skills, is why we shall train every day beginning tomorrow. Your strength is natural, my dove, but technique must be learned."

CHAPTER THREE

IN WHICH NICKIE NICK
MEETS HER FIRST VAMPIRE

The entire house was now sleeping soundly. I had tried to sleep. I really had tried, but my mind was reeling with images of ghosts and demons and vampires. I had put the wooden stake beneath my pillow, and I could feel it there. I mean, I couldn't actually feel it with my head through the fluffy down pillow, but I could *feel* it there, as if it called to something deep inside me. That same something was urging me to get up and go out into the night. It was a deep pressure, imploring me to hunt.

After a few hours, I gave into the call. My dingy boy's clothes were piled in with the laundry in the basement, so I dug them out and pulled them over my chemise and pantaloons. I twisted my long hair into a tight knot and put the cap over it. After smudging some dirt from the sleeve of my overcoat onto my cheeks and tucking my new stake into my belt, I was ready to head out.

I resisted the urge to take off my scarf, cap, and fingerless gloves while creeping through the hot kitchen on the way to the pantry and reminded myself how cold it would be outside in just a few more minutes.

And cold it was.

As soon as I opened the pantry window the wind howled, blowing snowflakes past me and onto the sink top on which I stood. As I went to hoist myself up through the window, I forgot about my new strength again and ended up bashing my head against the ceiling. A second attempt proved more successful, actually getting me through the window.

My foot stopped the window from crashing closed, then eased it almost all the way shut, propping it open with a stone kept nearby just for that purpose. Some heat would escape, but that stuffy basement could use some airing out. I thought about my boys and how cold they likely were tonight, wishing I could take some of our extra heat to them.

As I stepped out of our garden and into the adjacent alleyway, I marveled at the streets all decorated for Christmas, which was just a few days away. The snow fell steadily yet sparsely, a perfect grey night punctuated by the white flakes which were illuminated by the points of gaslights leading down the street.

We lived in a rather posh neighborhood in Lambeth, mostly middle-class, with a sprinkling of upper-class for further decoration. Father's textile factory was just across the Waterloo Bridge near the Thames's north bank, but the nearer bridge to our house was Westminster. From the south bank one could see the magnificent Houses of Parliament across the water. Always an impressive sight, they were even more so this time of year. With all the holiday decorations in the glow of the gaslights, it made the entire city look almost surreal, and my favorite time to see it was at night.

But I was heading in the opposite direction tonight. Just a few blocks away on the other side of Kennington Road was the Lambeth Workhouse, a horrid place. Conrad had told me stories about it, for he had been there shortly after his father had died and his mother forced into an asylum. I had known Conrad from our childhood. We had played at the textile factory together as children, because Fanny had to sometimes pitch in when my parents had been still struggling. She brought me along for a few hours and there were other workers' children there as well. Conrad and I hit it off from the start. But once the money started coming, they no longer allowed me to play with those beneath our station, as mother put it. They also did away with the day care for workers. My parents had reasoned that care for their workers' children should come out of the parents' pocket, not theirs. Still, Conrad and I had kept in touch over the years, especially after the accident. No forced sense of decorum could keep me away from my best friend.

Just a few more blocks from the workhouse was an abandoned warehouse, the current residence of Conrad and my other friends. That was, at least, until it was discovered they were there. They moved around mostly at night and in the early morning, so as not to be detected. It was not a great neighborhood anymore, and it could be quite dangerous at any time of day.

My disguise as a boy not only facilitated movement, because skirts and corsets certainly didn't allow one to move freely or quickly, but it also helped keep me safe. There were far more nasties to be done to a young woman than a young man on the dark streets of London. Although with my new strength, I shouldn't worry about that too much.

Still, I was sure to walk in my boy-walk, strutting with my feet turned out and hands in my pockets. It was the exact opposite I was expected to do as a lady, and I loved how carefree it felt.

"Well if it ain't Nickie Nick," a familiar voice came from a particularly dark alleyway.

I cringed. I hated when Conrad called me that, but of course, he called me that because he knew I hated it, so I said nothing. Conrad emerged, bundled up in a coat and scarf I had found for him. I often snagged things from my parents stash to bring down to Conrad and the others. After all, it was their fault he and the other boys were on the streets. The least they could do is provide some clothes for them.

"Conrad. I was just on my way to see you and the others. What are you doing out so late?"

"I might ask the same of you, Nickie."

"Shhhh!" I scolded and then whispered. "You know better than that when I'm dressed this way. Do you want me to be hurt? Nick, all right? Just Nick."

"There ain't nobody about, Nick. Relax. How was your fine party? Find a rich husband yet?" He threw a rather large pebble down the alley. I heard it skip once and then make a soft, wet sound, as if finding a new home in a pile of snow.

"Where are the boys? Are they inside?" I asked, ignoring his question. The annoyance in his voice I also chose to ignore.

"A-course," he said.

"Well, what are you waiting for? Let's go!"

"As you wish, m'lady," he quipped with a mocking bow.

A wave a nausea came over me and a man stood behind Conrad. It was as if he just had appeared out of nothing. I had heard no footsteps, had seen no movement. Just one moment he was there, and in the next he grabbed Conrad by the shoulders. He hissed at me and his pointed teeth caught the gaslight from the corner. Its face was quite horrid. It must have been really old, for it had only the faintest hint of human appearance.

After another moment, my mind registered that this was indeed a vampire, then I reacted without further thought. It was if my body knew what to do while my brain was still catching up. Before the vampire even got a fang in, I was on him. Knocking Conrad aside rather roughly with my left hand, I grabbed the stake out of my belt with my right and lunged at the vampire. My reaction took the horrid thing off guard, but not nearly enough. He deflected me and sent me in a somersault off to the side and the entire world was a blur until my head clunked on the snow-coved cobblestones and stars filled my vision. I rolled back to my feet an instant later, turning back to face it again.

But only Conrad remained.

"What the–" Conrad said, rubbing his head.

"Where did it go?" I took a moment to catch my breath and pushed the hair from my eyes. In my tumble, my cap had come off and my dark hair now spilled over my shoulders.

"I dunno," he answered and then followed with "Ow!" He rubbed his arm where I had knocked him out of the way and then rubbed his head again. He must have hit it on the street as well.

After twisting my hair back up under my cap I said, "Let us get off the streets."

He led me down the alley into the secret passageway behind some wooden crates. We went as quietly as possible through the walls and down the stairs until we reached the cellar where the boys stayed.

"Nick!" Edwin cried and ran to give me a big hug around the middle. Edwin was the youngest of the four boys and the most recently orphaned. His parents, like all of theirs, died in my parents' factory. There were always accidents with the machinery. The unluckiest were not the ones who died, however. The worst were the ones that were just maimed and could no longer work. They had no choice, either they go to a work-house or live on the streets. Still, perhaps the very worst of them all were the children left behind for those who did die. They had the same choice, workhouse or streets. According to Conrad, the streets were far better than the workhouse, which is why they all stuck together.

"Hey there, Ed." I stooped down to his height so I could give him a proper hug. He was such a sweet boy. Only nine years old with sandy blond hair and blue eyes. He had the face of an angel covered in dirt, which he almost always was. The clothes he wore were a little big on him. They were Rufus's old ones, since Rufus had outgrown them.

The basement was dank, damp, dark, and cold. There were only three lanterns, all of which I had snatched from my house. They kept the wicks low, so as not to waste the limited oil.

"Didja bring more food?" Rufus said from the floor where he and Edwin had just been playing a game of cards. Rufus was the second youngest at twelve.

"Not this time, but I will be sure to bring more in the morning," I replied, and I chastised myself for forgetting. There was just so much on my mind, and I had just come face to face with a vampire. Strange night all around.

"Hi Franklin," I addressed the boy huddling in the corner with a pile of junk. His head was down, and he was tinkering with something, as usual. Franklin had just turned fourteen, and he had an uncanny ability to turn junk into wondrous little working gadgets and machines. He often demonstrated some of his gadgets on the streets to help the boys make some money. Passersby would marvel at his mechanical toys and toss a few pennies his way.

"Oh." He looked up from his work, as if he was surprised anyone else was in the room. He was truly in his own world. "Hello Nick. All right?"

"I dunno about that," Conrad said. "What just happened up there, Nickie?"

What should I say? I mean, do I tell a group of homeless boys that there is even more danger out there than previously thought?

"Um," I started, quite eloquently. "It was a—" really? Can I explain this? If I couldn't tell my best friends, who could I tell? I took a deep breath and just blurt it out. "It was a vampire."

I waited for their laughter, but there was none. Well, none except for Conrad, who always scoffed at me. The other three just looked at me with wide eyes. Edwin eyes glistened with tears.

"A vampire. A-course it was, Nickie. Nah. It was just some old crazy guy, probably escaped from Bethlehem." Conrad plopped down on his bedroll, which consisted of some hay and rather worn bedding, and started whittling.

He was referring to Bethlehem Asylum just a few blocks away. He joked about it when he could. I suppose it was the only way for him to deal with it, as his mother was a patient there. She had gone mad after Conrad's father was killed at my parents' factory, an accident with the machinery. She just couldn't cope with the loss. They had adored each other, the way Conrad told the story. *When* Conrad told the story, which was almost never. He didn't like to relive that horror, and I couldn't blame him. After his mother was taken away, Conrad was sent to the workhouse, but he had escaped shortly thereafter. Since then we looked out for each other, and Conrad took it upon himself to help other boys who were orphaned in the same way. That was how he had gathered his small band of ruffians. They all worked together to survive, and I helped as much as I could.

"It was a vampire, Conrad," I asserted. "Turns out I'm rather the expert, as it were."

That statement was met with just blank stares, all except for Conrad, of course, who made another sneering sound and kept whittling.

"Fanny told me so, earlier tonight. She said I was *The Protector*. I fulfilled an old prophecy called The Hawthorn Legacy."

Again. Blank stares.

"Watch this." I grabbed the lantern Edwin and Rufus had been using. I turned up the wick to allow more light to spill into the basement, illuminating the grey stone walls and dirt floor.

It already felt warmer in the dingy basement, but oil was hard to come by.

After placing the lantern on a pile of scavenged wood, I took a rather large piece of broken beam. It was about as thick as my thigh, just about the same width as my bedpost, so this should do the trick.

All eyes were on me, even Conrad's, as I broke the wood over my knee. It splintered in two, and although it did hurt a little, the pain was gone as quickly as it had come.

"Woah!" the three younger ones sang in unison.

"What's going on, Nickie?" Conrad said, now standing again. He came over to me and took the wood out of my hands, probably inspecting it to see if it had been rotted through. He looked at me with wonder, mouth hanging open.

"Like I told you, I fulfill The Hawthorn Legacy. I have been chosen." I told them everything Fanny had explained to me, and no one interrupted me or scoffed this time, not even Conrad. They all just listened with rapt attention until I had finished.

Franklin said "Woah" again.

"I know. It is rather a lot to take in. Imagine how I feel." I sank down to the floor with them all. We sat for a few moments in silence, not really knowing what to say.

"So," Conrad started. "That thing up there was really a vampire? It was trying to, what, bite me?" He knew the answer without me having to speak it, and his face turned quite white upon that realization. "How have we lived on the streets so long and have never seen one before? I mean, we're out there every night and every day. Begging. Working. Winning food and such."

That was what they called it when they stole food, or anything. They said they had "won" it. Conrad also scavenged, and he was teaching Rufus to do so as well. They spent low tide down by the river as mudlarks, finding wood, coins, jewelry, bones, rags, and bits of copper. Anything that they could sell. Conrad alone worked as a tosher in the sewers doing the same. It was too dangerous for Rufus, but at fourteen, he would join him. Franklin's time was better spent tinkering, as his gadgets brought in as much as all the rest put together.

"I don't know," I said at a loss. "Lucky?"

Again, the familiar dismissive sound came from Conrad. "Right. 'Cause we are so lucky. Luck o'the devil," he mumbled.

"We *are* lucky," Edwin said. "We have Nick to look after us."

This made me smile, and it really moved me. I felt the tears forming, but I swallowed hard and didn't allow them to come. Now was no time for frivolous sentimentalities, especially with such danger afoot. Especially since...

"Or," I continued slowly, not wanting to even think it let alone say it. "Perhaps they can feel me. I mean, I certainly felt the change go through me. Fanny says that I should be able to learn to sense them, although I didn't feel anything except a little nauseous, maybe they can sense me, too."

"So, great." Conrad stood up and glowered down at me. "These bloodthirsty creatures of the night can *sense* you, and you led them straight to us."

CHAPTER FOUR

IN WHICH NICKIE NICK
LEARNS SOME MOVES

"You could have been killed!" Fanny yelled in a whispery voice, for we certainly couldn't risk my parents overhearing, not even in our big house. My father's office was just down the hall after all, and he was probably there. He was always there. Always working, unless he was at the factory.

"What were you thinking?" she continued.

"I was not thinking, Fanny." I sat at my dressing table and brushed my nose with some powder. "I went with my feeling, just like you said. My entire being was urging me to go out last night. It was like I needed to hunt, so I followed my instincts." I put some color on my cheeks and checked to see if they were evenly rosy in my dressing table mirror. Even, but subtle.

"I should have better prepared you, lassie," Fanny said, getting all teary-eyed as she fixed my hair for the day. After braiding it down my back, she twisted it around itself into a high bun. Her sleek red hair was pulled back into a tight bun at the nape of her neck, as usual, but her cheeks were more rosy than normal. Naturally rosy, no added color there. "I should have told you years ago, Nick. How could I have been so foolish?"

"That's not doing us any good now, Fanny." My tone sounded little more harsh than I had intended. I took a deep breath and smoothed some stray hairs back along the side behind my ear. My hair need not be perfect, after all. We were just going to train, whatever that meant.

She looked up at me shocked at my tone, but she got the message. "You are right," she said, moving across the room. "What's done is done. We shall train today. All day. Make up for lost time and all that. You shan't go out unprepared again."

"And where are we going to do this training, Fanny? In the garden for all of London to see me in my knickers? Or do you expect me to wear a corset and bustle and carry a parasol as well as a stake?"

"In the attic, actually," she responded, ignoring my quip about the bustle. "I had Wilfred start on clearing a space to train last night. He worked through the night, as I impressed upon him the importance of it."

"You told *Wilfred*?" I asked incredulously. Wilfred was one of the lower butlers of the household. He was around Fanny's age, and I had always suspected he was sweet on her. Now I knew for sure.

Really. A woman of her age. She was so old, like forty-something. How unseemly.

"We can trust Wilfred." Each time she said his name, her voice softened just a little. "He follows the old ways as well. Just you leave him to me." She blushed, as if she knew what I had been thinking. "Let's get you dressed," she continued, holding up a day skirt and corset. "I got one of your mother's corsets for the time being. I sent Judith out today to get you a larger one of your own. If last night proved anything, it is that you cannot wear a corset that tight anymore. Not only can I not cinch it properly, but you were lucky you didn't bust the seams simply by breathing. No, you must still wear one, of course." She likely saw the joy on my face at the thought of not wearing one. "Just not quite so tight. It might make you less desirable for your potential husbands, however, adding a few inches to your waist."

"Good!" I exclaimed without hesitation. "Perhaps it will deter The Most Annoying One, too. Can we just make me look downright frumpy? I shall eat many more apple tarts with great pleasure." I smirked, waiting for Fanny's response.

"Let us not go overboard, my dear. You will lose your figure soon enough, no need to rush it." She patted her own waistline as an example.

Fanny was not fat by any means, but she was on the plump side. I liked it. It was so much more freeing that watching every little thing one ate, as mother insisted. Mother likely would not be too happy about this waistline increase, but it was all so trivial after all. It was my waist regardless, nothing actually changed there. The only difference was how much we forced it into being reduced in a corset. So now instead of reducing it five inches, it will only be two or three. Fine by me. I rather liked to breathe.

"Take hold of the bedpost." She indicated the one that was not the broomstick tied with twine. "Just not too tightly," she added through a wide grin.

She began to put me into mother's corset, which was not all that much larger than my old ones. After all, she was still a fine-looking woman, nearly as old as Fanny. But after giving birth to me, her waist would never be reduced to fourteen inches again. My waist had never been fourteen inches, since I stood a few inches taller than her. Mother was a very tiny woman, a full head shorter than me. She would tell stories of how father used to be able to encircle her waist with his hands back when they first met. Now she settled for twenty inches, which was a dream for me, as I usually was forced into a corset that made my waist eighteen inches. But only reduced to twenty inches? Only a three inch reduction!

I might even be able to fight vampires in a corset like that.

Lacing the larger corset was far more successful. No more broken bedposts. After putting me in an under bustle, meant to hold out the ruffles on the back of a walking skirt, and a simple day skirt and blouse, she led me up to the fourth floor.

No one ever went up to the fourth floor, certainly not my parents. It had been used mostly for storage, and we called it an attic. The third floor was mostly for servant rooms and the like. The second is where my family lived and where father's office was. The library, dining room, and parlor were all on the first floor, street level. Then the kitchen, pantry, laundry, and more was on the basement level. It was quite a large house, and I got a little nauseous every time I thought about how much unused space we had and how little space my four misfortunate friends had.

"Wow," I said as we reached the fourth floor. Granted, I had not been up there for quite some time, but it had been completely transformed.

Wilfred swept up the last bit of dust and dirt into a bin.

"Miss Hawthorn." He bowed formally. "I hope it is to your liking." His eyes twinkled at Fanny, and she blushed again.

"It is amazing, Wilfred! You did all this in one night?"

Boxes upon boxes were piled neatly in the corners. Some of my old toys and a faded rocking horse were there. Old dolls with missing eyes and torn dresses sat primly along the tops of the crates in a neat row. More trunks and old furniture were piled in other corners and along the walls. Most of the interior walls had been removed on this half of the house by the former owners, so it was a large, open space with few supporting beams here and there. In the center of the room was a heavy wooden stand, padded with old pillows and tied around the middle with some twine that looked suspiciously like the kind holding my bed together.

"That's to practice your–um–scrappin' skills." He pointed to the padded wooden stand. He demonstrated by throwing a punch right into the heart of the pillow. "See? Practice dummy. Protects yer hands," he continued.

I wanted to run and hug him, but that would not be proper, so I just folded my hands over my skirt and with a courteous nod said, "Thank you, Wilfred. Thank you so much for this."

"Yes. You did a wonderful job." Fanny's voice had a softness to it that I rarely heard other than when she spoke of him. They exchanged another smile, like it was a secret.

"Well," Wilfred said. "I shall leave you ladies to it. Let me know if I can be of any more service." With a tip of his cap, he left the room.

Fanny didn't speak until we heard his footfalls start down the stairs.

"This will most certainly do." She spoke to no one in particular. After surveying the room again, she turned to me and continued, "Now, tell me again of your encounter last night."

"Like I said, it was over quite quickly. He was not there, then he was. I reacted. He deflected. I hit the cobblestones. He was gone," I summarized. "That's about it, and it happened just about that fast, too."

"Show me." She indicated that I should demonstrate on the practice dummy Wilfred had made.

"Are you serious?"

"Quite."

I pulled out the stake which I had put down the front of my corset, as I couldn't be seen walking through the house with a stake (although, I would have to find a better way to carry it), and lunged at the dummy.

"Yes," Fanny said. "I see your mistake. Your balance was off. The sheer force of you lunging forward swinging the stake thus gave the creature much time to react. Indeed. You are quite lucky to be alive."

"Much time? It all happened in an instant!"

"Yes, an instant in your perception, but the creature can move at a different speed. This is why he seemed to just 'appear,' as you said."

"Well, how can I kill a vampire who moves faster than I can even see?"

"You cannot see it yet," she said. "Yet is the key word there, my dear. Your strength came upon you quickly and you were unable to control it, but you are already adjusting to that, no?"

"Yes. I'm getting better already." I demonstrated by lunging toward the practice dummy again, paying close attention to how my body felt. "I can use the extra strength when I need to, but I can adjust my actions to fit normal life as well. Or, at least, door handles are no longer coming off in my hand. That's progress, isn't it?"

"Perfect. Your other senses and abilities will need rather more concentration to tap into and to control, Nicole. They will not be as apparently easy as the strength. The Protector has many abilities, and you have not even scratched the surface of yours. You had a taste of heightened senses when you first transformed, remember? But now you must learn to hone those. With some practice, you will be as fast as a vampire when you need to be. That's why we are here, training. To learn. Now again, only this time, try to remember what you felt, not only what you saw."

I thought for a moment, replaying last night's brief encounter again in my mind. I slowed it down, trying to analyze every moment. There was something.

"I felt nauseous, then something moved me to action. It was like my body knew what to do, although, I guess it really didn't after all."

Perhaps I was lucky to be alive.

"That feeling is the essence of your power." Fanny put a clenched fist to her stomach for emphasis. "You feel the urge, and it may feel like nausea now, but that's only because you have nothing else to compare it to. It might also feel similar to nervousness or excitement, but you must hone your attention to this feeling to differentiate between the subtleties of it."

"How do you know all this, Fanny?" She'd been a governess for seventeen years, how could she possibly know about the subtleties of The Protector's powers?

"As I told you, I was chosen among those in my coven to care for you, in case you were the Hawthorn to fulfill The Legacy, but there were other possibilities for The Protector as well. I was trained to guide The Protector since I was a girl, knowledge and skills handed down through generations. It is why I used to fight vampires to learn how so I could teach you. You, my dear, will be the strongest of all the Protectors, however, because of your heritage. Because of the blessing the witches put upon your family."

"Blessing?"

"Some would say curse, but it depends on one's perspective, doesn't it? After what your ancestor did at the

Salem Witch Trials, condemning so many women to horrible deaths, the coven demanded retribution, but not in the way of punishment, in the way of service. You see?"

"So I'm cursed." I felt rather angry.

"Do you feel cursed?" Fanny asked wisely. She folded her hands over her belly and waited for my answer.

"No," I said after a few moments of checking in with my body. "I feel magnificent, like I could do anything. Like I never even have to sleep again. The energy surging through me is without end. Power without limits."

"Well, my dear. There are limits, as there should be. You will also need to sleep, although likely not as much as most, which will certainly facilitate you leading a double life. Which you, of course, will have to lead, my dear. And no one will be able to know your identity."

"Well...." I looked down, embarrassed. "I–I already told someone."

Fanny sighed and shook her head. "Let me guess. Conrad. You told Conrad already?"

"He was there, Fanny," I protested. "The vampire tried to bite him on the neck." I thrust two fingers in the shape of a "v" towards my throat to dramatize my point. "What was I supposed to tell him happened?"

"Indeed."

"And..." I started.

Fanny looked at me sharply, crossing her arms the way she did when she was rather cross with me.

"The other boys know, too." Before she could scold me, and I saw that she was about to with the deep breath she had just taken, I continued, "But just those four, I promise. No one else knows, well except Wilfred. Ah ha!" I pointed the wooden stake at her, feeling justified. "You told Wilfred, so obviously people can know."

"Yes, well, Wilfred is"–Fanny blushed again–"a very good friend." She relaxed her arms and rubbed her neck.

"Is that what you call it?"

I was lucky she didn't take me over her knee for being so cheeky. But she just smiled. I guess I was all grown up now.

"Enough, little mite," she snickered. That was what she has called me since I was a girl. I guess I was not all that grown up in her eyes, nor would I ever be. "No one else, all right?"

"All right. As if anyone would believe me anyway."

"Back to training, my dear girl. Stand before the beast as you did last night."

I did as she asked, but then she pushed me and I stumbled to catch my balance.

"Fanny!"

"Point proven? Here, stand like this." She positioned me in a way that my legs were spread and knees bent. My arms out before me, protecting my torso. Stake out.

"Feel the strength here." She put her hand just below my navel. "Feel the floor beneath you, Nick. Feel how your feet are one with the floor. With the house. With the earth. Can you feel that?"

It sounded all rather silly, but I just suspended my skepticism for a moment, and I really could feel it. For lack of a better word, it felt all tingly. Like tiny bits of light and strength was coming up through the soles of my shoes into my feet and running up through my body. It felt much as the fire that coursed through my body last night, when the change had come upon me.

I didn't realize I had closed my eyes to concentrate until Fanny had pushed me again, but this time I didn't budge.

"This is the difference," she said. "Now from this position of stability and power, you move."

I tried the move again and thrust the stake at the stationary dummy, driving into his fluffy, feathered breast. It splintered the wood behind the pillow with a loud crack.

"I can certainly feel the difference, Nanny, but how will this help if the vampire is moving at lightening speed?"

"Trust the process, my dear. It will become evident."

CHAPTER FIVE

IN WHICH NICKIE NICK
MEETS HIM

The crackling fire both illuminated my book and warmed my skirts. I sat curled up on my father's favorite comfy reading chair with a book. It was an adventure story about a woman cadet in the Royal Air Navy, and I dreamed I was her. Just last week the Times had a drawing of such a woman, dressed smartly with spats and trousers. Her waist was cinched with a utility corset and she had on a tiny bustle, as that was the uniform for women, but she was powerful. Her strong stance in the drawing showed that. She looked proudly out from under her flight cap, goggles perched on her forehead. As I read, I dreamed of joining the RAN instead of living this frivolous life. If mother forced me to marry Lord Fouffypants Godwyn, I would.

But for now, it was enough just to dream of grand adventures while reading about them in front of the fire. It was the best way to spend a cold December evening, especially when my parents were out, as they were tonight. They went to another Christmas dinner, then a party afterwards. Fortunately for me, Fanny convinced them I was unwell, so I got to stay home. No doubt His Most Insolent and Annoying would be there, and I was in no mood for talking marriage with him or any other beau. Reginald Godwyn would do well to find himself a wife who would obey and serve him, and I would do well to be left alone.

My legs were rather sore from the day of training. Fanny had really surprised me with her knowledge of hand-to-hand combat. She not only taught me how to focus and center myself, but she also showed me some amazing moves. However, every time I had kicked the pillow-padded dummy, my skirt would get all tangled up around my legs. And that skirt had been a simple one. How would I ever fight vampires efficiently in a proper skirt, not to mention bustle and petticoats as well.

"What are you doing?" Fanny queried from behind me as she entered the library. The top of her skirt was balled up in her fists, and she rushed over to me, heels clunking on the hardwood floor. A few stray red hairs framed her rosy cheeks.

I held up my book. "Reading."

"You don't have the luxury of reading anymore, girl. You need to be out there, especially now they know you exist. And, with your blunder last night, they think The Protector is an inept and foolish girl."

"Tonight? But it is the day before Christmas Eve, and I have trained all day. Surely the vampires can wait until after Christmas."

"The vampires will not wait, and neither shall you. You must find and kill a vampire tonight, dear girl. If you don't, there is no telling what kind of Christmas it will be. Up! Up with you. Go change. You are going out. Why do you think I lied to your parents for you? The Protector does not get a night off, my dear. Go up and change."

I slammed the book shut and dropped it on the floor with a thud. "This is so unfair! I didn't ask for this!" I shouted, standing up with balled, angry fists at my side. I knew I sounded childish, and at the moment, I just didn't care.

Fanny picked up the book from the floor and patted my bustle with it. "Upstairs with you to change. It is your duty now."

"Fine." I stormed out of the room and up the stairs. There in my chamber my boy's clothes were laid out, clean for a change. The clumpy boots lay next to my bed. I dressed quickly, trading my blouse and skirt for a shirt, waistcoat, and trousers. I twisted my hair up into my cap, put on the boots and overcoat, and stomped back out of the room just as Fanny was coming in.

"Forgetting something?" she asked, picking up the wooden stake from my bed. "You would not want to be caught without that tonight," she said, softer now.

I rolled my eyes and snatched the stake from her, but Fanny had some speed of her own. She caught my arm before I could pull it away. There was strength in her as well. She looked at me with fierce, but kind, eyes. I immediately felt more calm.

"I know this is all rather new and quite the change in your life, my dear." Her words soothed me. I felt inexplicably serene. "You see," she continued, noticing my change in countenance, "I have some power of my own."

"But the necklace...I thought..."

"It does protect you against mind control, my lamb, but I'm appealing to your emotions. To your heart."

"What else can you do?"

With a wave of her hand, she mended the bedpost. The broom handle floated off to the side and the broken post that had been shoved under the bed rose up to take its place. Purple steam swirled around it, and it was like new. She flicked her hand toward the broken doorknob, and repaired it, too.

"You really are a witch!" I gaped at her. My sweet, Scottish nanny. She had hid all this power from me and worked as a servant all these years.

"We must work together as a team, my dear. You must go out there tonight with a clear head, focused. Otherwise, it could be the end of you. As I told you, that vampire normally would not have let you go last night. You had the element of surprise on your side, but you no longer have that. Tonight, they might be hunting you." She paused for a moment and her eyes turned sad. "And your friends."

"What? But they are just children. They have nothing to do with any of this."

"Do you think vampires care about that? Get out there. Stay hidden. Move fast, Nick."

Before she even finished her thought, I had pulled out of her grasp and was halfway down the back stairs. Once in the street, I pulled my scarf and gloves out of the pockets of my brown overcoat. The cold bit into my cheeks and stung my nose, but I moved so quickly that I warmed up soon enough. I had to get to the boys. They had to move. Tonight.

Nothing happened on the trip to the boys' shelter. I went in the secret passage way behind the crates and made my way into their cellar chamber. All but Conrad were there.

"Where is Conrad?" I asked, startling the three younger boys who had not seen me enter. "He is usually not out this late, is he? It is dangerous out there, doesn't he know that?"

"He'll be back soon," Rufus answered. "He said he wouldn't be long."

"Where did he go, Rufus?"

"I dunno. To find some food for us," he responded with a shrug, and I cursed myself for forgetting to bring them food again.

Franklin was in the corner, working on something with metal. I looked over at Conrad's bedroll, and there were about a dozen or so wooden stakes.

"Did he go to hunt vampires?" I pointed to the stakes on the floor.

"No." Edwin had been quiet until now, and looking at him, I could see why. My tales of vampires yesterday mixed with my current agitated state had frightened the poor boy. He was sitting against the wall with his arms tightly wrapped around his legs. "He made those for you."

Taking a deep breath, I forced myself to relax. "Come here."

Edwin got up and walked over to me, never taking his eyes off the dirt floor. I stooped down to his height and lifted his chin. "It is all right, dear boy. I'm here now, and I shan't let anything happen to you." My reassurances did little to convince myself of my supposed ability to keep them safe, but Edwin seemed to believe me. He threw his arms around my neck and hugged me.

I thought it best to change the subject away from vampires until Conrad returned. No need to scare these boys into thinking he was in danger, although he likely was. The call deep within my core swelled, telling me to get outside and guard the perimeter of the building, but I had to soothe them first, especially since my heated entrance had just done more to upset them.

Franklin worked feverishly in the corner, so I went over to him with Edwin under my arm. Rufus followed and sat down near Franklin. "What are you working on today?"

"It's something for you, too," he said. "Conrad and I decided last night after you left, that we were gonna help you. We all will help, however we can."

My heart warmed at this, but something else crept up my throat. Fear. I had put all these boys in danger. Now I must deter them from this task without alarming them, but I didn't know how.

"What is it?" I tried to think of what else to say, knowing that I had to get upstairs and keep watch. The call in my gut pulled at me to leave, but I remained.

"It is a surprise, a birthday surprise," he said with a smile. I looked over a Rufus who was now sitting with his hand around Edwin.

"Rufus, get out your cards and deal a game for you and Edwin. I'm going to go up and wait for Conrad for a bit. You two play a game, and when I get back, I shall play, too. Deal?" I smiled, and hoped they couldn't sense the growing dread in my belly.

"Deal!" Edwin loved when I played cards with them, so perhaps that will keep their mind off things while I go upstairs. "Franklin, you all right?"

Franklin didn't answer with words. He just nodded and continued working away. He didn't like to be disturbed from his work.

When I was out of their sight, I broke into a run up the stairs, my belly screaming at me now. As soon as I poked my head through the secret passageway opening, I heard it. A scuffle. Right here in the alley. I jumped out, grabbing the stake out of my belt, and I saw Conrad fighting with one vampire and someone else fighting with another. Conrad reared back and clocked the vampire on the jaw with the fist grasping one of his stakes. I heard Conrad's sharp intake of breath at the pain, then smelled the blood at the same moment the vampire did. It was an awful, strong and sickly copper smell that undesirably mixed with my growing nauseous Protector senses, and I suppressed a retch.

The vampire had the opposite reaction. Its face became feral and he lunged at Conrad.

I moved, but my feet got tripped up on my oversized boy's boots. Recovering quickly, I rushed forward, stake at the ready and tackled the vampire, who already had Conrad pinned to the ground. Its teeth sunk into his skin just before I reached them. Rolling the vampire off Conrad, I miraculously ended up on top after the tumble and, without hesitation, thrust the stake right through the heart. It was if my body acted on its own again. My conscious mind had not caught up until all that was beneath me was a body-shaped pile of brown dust. I looked up at Conrad who was against the stone wall, holding his neck. Blood was oozing between his fingers and the look on his face was one of sheer terror.

The other man was still fighting the other vampire. It was mostly a blur, but after one rather fierce kick to the chest that sent the vampire flying back against the opposite alley wall, the man looked at me with his hand out and said, "Stake, please?"

For a moment, I was caught by his dark eyes, which looked familiar somehow, and couldn't move, but fortunately my body reacted again where my mind couldn't. My arm tossed him the stake. Not a moment after he caught it, he rammed it into the chest of the charging vampire.

Dust.

The young man looked at me crossly and tossed the stake aside. It stuck in the snow piled in the corner of the alley, making it look as if a large wooden-nosed snowman had wilted there. What a curious thought.

"Are you all right," the man said to Conrad, kneeling beside the both of us.

Conrad tried to speak, but only gurgling noises came out. He was getting paler by the moment.

The man ripped off the ascot from around his neck and put it over Conrad's throat wound. I could see (and smell) that the blood had already started to slow. There were two perfectly round puncture wounds.

"Keep pressure on it," the man commanded. His eyes were dark, like coal, and it matched his black hair. Long black sideburns came down and barely touched his strong jaw. Soot was smeared over his face, but even so, he was the most beautiful thing I had ever seen. He was the man from the window last night. The excitement mounting in my stomach confirmed it.

I reached out to hold the ascot in place, and as I touched his hand a thrill went through my core and I literally caught my breath. He pulled his hand from mine and backed away, wiping his mouth and smearing some of the soot away from his lips. They were the color of cinnamon, and the surrounding flesh was fair. I couldn't take my eyes from him.

"What are you playing at?" He looked down at me.

I blinked, rather taken aback from his tone.

"Look, boy, this is no place for children," he scolded. "Get your friend and get inside. Don't come out again at night." He pointed his finger at me as if he was my father and I a petulant child. Anger replaced the dreamy desire quite quickly. Who was he to call me 'boy'? He couldn't be but a year or so older than I was.

"No you look, sir. I held my own." I pointed to the body-shaped pile of dust.

"You got lucky."

"Lucky! I'm *The–*." I almost said Protector, but Fanny's words came back to me how no one else could know.

"Nick." Conrad's voice sounded so weak. "Are they gone?"

My attention turned back to Conrad. "Yes. Gone." When I turned back to face my handsome stranger, he was gone. "Let's get you inside."

Conrad got up with my help. He must have lost more blood than I thought, as his shirt was soaked with it and he leaned heavily on me in his weakness. The smell was horrible. No doubt due to my new super power senses, I suppose. After all, I had been around blood before, but it never smelled like this. Perhaps it was to facilitate the recognition of danger or the presence of vampires feeding. The thought made me shudder. Seeing Conrad pinned beneath that vampire had been truly frightening, and rather disgusting. These creatures were repulsive parasites, and I suddenly felt quite proud that I was chosen to help rid the world of them. They deserved to die, and I looked forward to dusting as many of them as I could.

CHAPTER SIX

IN WHICH NICKIE NICK
SEES A RICKETT

The two younger boys looked up from their card game as Conrad and I entered the room. Their fear-filled eyes wide at the sight of the blood. Edwin started to cry silently.

"He will be all right." I helped Conrad over to his bedroll. "It is just a scratch from a fight. Really, Edwin, it is not as bad as it looks." I tried to be reassuring, but I turned to see three very uncomforted boys. "Really," I said again. "He shall be just fine."

They had all gathered rather close behind me to watch. I pulled up the beautiful stranger's ascot and looked. The blood had stopped flowing. At the moment it was just a light ooze.

"Rufus, I need you to hold this tight on Conrad's neck, all right?"

"No," Conrad interrupted. "I can do it myself." He smiled despite the pain and looked up at me with a softness I had not seen before. He looked at me the same way I had felt when I looked at that beautiful stranger.

Flustered, I got up quickly and stumbled on my oversized boots again. "Curse these boots!" I said, kicking them off. I can hardly walk in these clodhoppers let alone fight.

Franklin went back to his corner, picked up a piece of coal and started sketching something on the wall. The entire corner of the room was covered with his coal-sketched drawings, the first manifestation of his creations. Each of those drawings someday would be made into some amazing gadget pieced together with scavenged items from the streets.

"Are you all right, Nickie?" Edwin wiped away his tears. He saw the blood on my shirt collar, but I convinced him I was fine by taking off my coat and showing him my neck. Looking down, I noticed my waistcoat was shredded over my stomach, so I unbuttoned it and discovered that the shirt beneath it was shredded as well. The vampire must have lashed out at me just before he dusted. Fanny had said they had rather claw-like fingernails.

I felt beneath the shirt to see if my chemise was also ripped, but my hand touched something hard. The corset. In my rush to get dressed I had forgotten to take it off. Never did I think that I would forget about a corset. Good thing, too, as it likely saved my life tonight, or at least kept me from being slashed and wounded.

"Listen boys," I started, still marveling at my luck two nights in a row. If I had had any doubt about the importance of training, that doubt was all gone. "Get some rest for a few hours and then gather your things. You are moving in the morning."

"Moving? Where?" Rufus said. "Don't you remember how long it took for us to find this place?"

"I know, and I'm sorry, Rufus. It just is not safe here anymore."

"It is safer in here than on the streets," he protested.

"You will not be on the streets. We shall think of something," I reassured.

"I found another place earlier today," Conrad said weakly from his corner. "It's smaller than this, but it's safe. They won't know we're there. Unless, of course, you lead them to us again, Nickie."

Nausea. And it was not that vampire-is-near feeling, this was true nausea. It had been my carelessness that put them in this situation, but how was I to know? "I must get back out there, all right? We will move in the morning, after the sun comes up. That will be the safest time."

I turned to leave, but Conrad stopped me.

"Here." He grabbed a handful of carved stakes with his free hand, the other still held the ascot in place. He tossed the stakes to me and they all fell just at my feet on the earthen floor. Stooping to pick them up, I smiled. He had made all these for me.

When I looked back up at him to thank him, his eyes were once again full of love, so I turned away towards the others, not knowing what to do. Perhaps it was just because he was injured and afraid to die, but Conrad and I had been friends our whole lives. This just would not do.

"I shall keep watch tonight," I said, looking around at the four boys. "Then in the morning, I will go home to change and get some food. All right? Then move you to Conrad's new place."

Rufus grabbed one of the stakes from Conrad's bedside. "I'm coming with you."

"Oh no you are not," I replied in a tone that should have indicated there was to be no argument.

"I can fight." He puffed his chest out.

"No, Rufus. Not tonight. Not without any training, and even then. It is just too dangerous." His face fell and he turned, throwing the stake against the floor. He went to his own bed mat and plopped down, arms crossed.

"Let us all just get through the night, shall we? We will talk more about fighting and strategy tomorrow. Just get some rest, and take care of Conrad."

After tucking all the new stakes into my belt and any free pocket (I even put one down my corset), I grabbed my overcoat and headed back outside.

The alley was quiet this time when I emerged, and the smell of the blood was fading in the freshly falling snow. I went up to the mouth of the alley and stood just out of the light from the nearby gaslamp. The night had barely begun and the streets were rather busy with carriages and full of the sounds of clopping hoofbeats. My mind went back to the beautiful stranger. Where had he come from? Where had he gone to? One hears stories about how something very bad could be happening in an alleyway just adjacent a very busy street, but no one comes to help. I found that hard to believe before tonight.

Yet he had come to help. He had probably saved Conrad's life.

And he knew vampires existed, that was a definite benefit.

Then the strangest contraption caught my eye. It was a carriage without a horse, clattering down the street with the rest of the carriages. Being the daughter of industrialists, I certainly was not ignorant of modern machinery. After all, mother and father had some quite impressive steam machines that facilitated production in their textile factory. Even Franklin himself came up with truly ingenious inventions just from assembling junk and such, but this was like nothing I had ever seen up close. It looked every bit like a carriage, only instead of four wheels, it only had three, two large ones in back and a smaller one in front. From the large back wheels, chains ran from gears on the wheels to other gears extending from an axle beneath the carriage's floor. A man sat on the right, fully dressed for the evening in a top hat and fine overcoat, holding onto the steering rod with his left hand and another lever with his right. A woman wrapped in a fur stole and earmuffs sat beside him.

Stepping up to get a closer look as the thing puttered by, I saw that there was a mechanism beneath the carriage floor that turned the gears, which in turn, turned the wheels. I stooped down to get a look of the thing from beneath, but it had already passed. There on the back sat the engine. It looked like a coal boiler and a long pipe extending up from it belched out steam.

"Interesting, no? A far cry from a penny-farthing," a smooth voice above me said. I stood up quickly to find that it was none other than my beautiful stranger.

"Yes. It is a Rickett Carriage. I read about them, but I have never seen one before. Simply amazing," I responded calmly, although some rather large fluttery things had taken up residence in my stomach.

"You read, do you? Also interesting. This evening is just full of surprises, is it not, Nick?"

"How do you know my name." It came out as a whisper, for I was breathless. He filled my world. It was as if all of London fell away from my vision, and there was only him. Black eyes twinkling in the gaslight. One side of his cinnamon lips curled up in a half-smile. Pale skin covered in soot and jaw-hugging sideburns. I shivered, and it was not the cold December night that caused it.

"Your friend said it before. It is beneficial to pay attention to the details in life, don't you find? I am called Ashe." He offered a gloved hand. "We were not properly introduced before."

I took his hand and gave it a manly shake, which was not too difficult with my new strength.

"Strong, too, for such a young lad," he said, putting his hand back in his pocket.

I felt my brows furrow at this. He thought me a boy, and a kid at that. I was no kid. I was The Protector, after all.

"I'm not all that young." I deepened my voice perhaps a little too much. My cheeks suddenly felt very hot and flushed, so I turned my face into the cold wind and let the snowflakes cool my no-doubt-rosy-cheeks down. "Bet I'm as old as you."

Great. That sounded quite mature, Nicole.

"Do you now?" he said. "Thought I told you to stay safe and inside. This is no place for children. Where is your friend. Is he all right?"

I bit my lip to stop from scolding this infuriating man, and I turned back to him, ready to do so anyway. As soon as I caught his eyes again, however, I was unable to speak. Literally. The ability to form words completely escaped me.

"He is all right, isn't he?" He sounded concerned.

I couldn't even manage a simple 'yes,' so I nodded instead.

"So, tell me more about this Rickett Carriage, Nick." Ashe leaned casually against the stone wall of the building but kept his dark eyes scanning the streets.

"Um." I tried to force my eyes off of him so I could at least speak again. Imitating him, I, too, leaned against the building and looked out at the passing carriages. "It was first built something like twenty years ago by this man named Thomas Rickett, an inventor of sorts, but it didn't go far. Now that technology has caught up with his vision, his original design has been taken by a new inventor and redesigned. It was just released last week." I felt his eyes boring into me. My face flushed again, and I tried to focus on my breath as Fanny had taught me.

"Impressive, Nick." His eyes shifted back to the street, and I breathed easier.

"He will be fine," I said, finally able to talk properly. "Conrad, the boy who was hurt. He will be just fine. The bleeding stopped and the others are caring for him below."

"And you?" he asked.

"Quite well," I answered a little too quickly.

"Your first vampire was it?" he asked.

"No. Last night was the first." Then I wondered why I was telling him anything. He was a stranger after all.

"You certainly knew what to do." He sounded rather impressed. "How does such a young boy know how to slay a vampire?"

There was that word again. I was not young. I mean, I was not old either, but the condescending way he said 'young' really irked me.

"I have been around" was my only response.

He made a noise that sounded like a stifled laugh, and I look up fiercely at him, ready to give it to him this time, but the words were once again caught in my throat. He was smiling, which should have only made me more furious, but it was the sweetest smile I had ever seen. It was like it was suddenly morning, as everything seemed brighter. A few snowflakes had gotten caught in his sideburns, and there, one fell on his lip.

"Well, Nick," he said, still smiling. "You seem to have everything under control here. Have a good night." He tipped his cap, showing me the momentary black curls beneath, and then he was gone.

I watched him walk away down the street, until a group of awkwardly marching men blocked Ashe from my view. I found myself hoping I would see him again.

CHAPTER SEVEN

IN WHICH NICKIE NICK
GETS SOME GADGETS

I arrived home shortly after dawn, and Fanny was waiting for me in the garden.

"Oh thank goodness," she said, and she gathered me up in her arms. "I feared the worst." She kissed the top of my cap several times, and then holding me at arm's length she added, "but I should have had more faith in you, my turtledove. Quick, get inside. The house is not yet stirring. Thankfully, your parents had a late night at their festivities."

It was Christmas Eve.

"Well," Fanny said, prompting me to speak as we entered my chamber. "How did it go last night? Did you get one?"

"I did." I took off my overcoat.

Fanny gasped when she saw my shredded shirt and waistcoat.

"I'm fine," I assured her. "I shall tell you all about it after I get some rest later this morning. Believe it or not, my corset saved me." I removed the ruined clothes down to my corset and camisole. The lace was snagged, but the boning held true. "Remind me of this the next time I complain about wearing one. I do like this larger size, though Fanny. Added protection and comfort. I had completely forgotten I still had it on."

"I have to speak with Judith my dear. Get into bed and rest for a few hours. I can cover for you until at least noon." She grabbed me in a big embrace and covered my forehead in a rapid succession of tiny kisses again. "Get some rest," she repeated.

I looked at myself in the looking glass, and I was a sight. Half-undressed, wearing just a chemise, corset, and boys dungarees. Long strands of hair were falling out from beneath my cap, and I hoped beyond hope I had not looked thus when speaking with Ashe last night. Something better must be done with my hair. Perhaps I could get Fanny to plait it tonight before heading out, then it will be less likely to fall out. After kicking off those horrid clodhopper boots and removing my trousers, I crawled into bed and fell asleep almost immediately. What seemed like only a few moments later, Fanny was shaking me awake.

"Wake up, Nicole. Your parents have gone out shopping, and your friend Conrad stopped by. He left you this." She placed a poorly wrapped package in front of me. "He said he moved the boys and that they were all safely in a new place now. The poor lad looked quite weak, so I sent him off with some food and a loaf of bread to share with the others."

"Thank you, Fanny. Yes. He got hurt last night. Vampire attack, but I dusted it."

"Good gracious!" she exclaimed. "Poor boy!"

"Did he say where their new place was?" I asked, then yawned. I really wanted to be still asleep. So much for needing less rest.

"He didn't, but he did say he would come back this evening," she said, and then added as I was about to protest, "before dusk, he said."

"How did I get them all mixed up into this, Fanny? How did I get mixed up into this?"

"Enough about that now. Open your gifts. This one from the boys, and this one"–she pulled a rather large package up from beneath the bed, better wrapped–"is from me. Something I had Janice make special for you this morning while you slept, along with the few things I had her get yesterday. Happy Christmas, Nicole. I know it is a bit early, but you will need them tonight."

I smiled at her and opened her gift. Inside, there were several pieces of clothing that looked quite similar to an airship cadet's uniform, just like I had read about and seen drawn in the newspaper. Only these were black instead of brown. First, I removed a black lace blouse and a pair of black trousers, but they were not nearly as baggy or clumsy as my boy's trousers had been. They looked almost like Mrs. Bloomers cycling trousers, which I had seen only in drawings. Frivolous things, but these were much less baggy. They looked to come down to about mid-calf. Since they were made for the active lives of female cadets, I would most certainly be able to fight in them.

Next in the box was a corset, but it was unlike any corset I had ever seen. It was made of black leather. Like a normal corset, it had busk fasteners on the front and laced down the back, but there also was a leather loop sewn into the side of it and a small pocket near the front of it, rather like the pocket of a waistcoat. Then a series of smaller loops lined the bottom right side of it. Quite a strange looking thing, and I couldn't imagine how one would wear such a contraption.

Next were the regulation mini-bustle and knee-high spats. It all looked exactly like the drawing in the paper along with the article about how the RAN introduced the mini-bustle for their female cadets. It was even sillier and more frivolous than actual bustles, but at least my derriere would be covered. The spats laced up the front and would do quite well to cover my ankles.

There at the bottom of the box was a new coat. It, too, was black, made from a very heavy, oilcloth, and as I took it out of the box, it just kept coming. I couldn't believe just how long it was, and it was lovely. Styled after a slender evening coat, but it was heavier somehow. This was not part of the RAN standard uniform, but it was quite glorious just the same.

I looked up at Fanny, not sure what to say. This was all quite generous, and they were exactly what I needed.

"They are for the night, my dear. Black, so you shan't easily be seen. Go on, try them on. They are patterned after a woman's airship uniform, so you will not stand out. Too much," she added. "I had the idea after I saw you reading that book yesterday. You would have to have something you could both fight in as well as mask your identity. You will see. Go on, then. What are you waiting for?"

I got up and began to dress, starting with the black lace blouse. It had a proper high collar, but upon closer inspection, the collar was lined with some sort of metal, so that when I fastened it, it had a metal collar to protect my neck.

These were vampire slaying clothes.

More excited now, I put on the trousers next, and then Fanny helped me get into the unique corset. It was stiff yet bendable, if that makes sense. The boning felt quite different.

Fanny saw me running my hand up the boned seams and said, "Military grade steel boning. Strong and flexible."

I rapped on the side of the corset with my fist and it almost felt and sounded solid. But I bent around in ever direction and even tried a kick or two. The thing didn't hinder my movement at all, not even a little bit. Then I examined the strange loops sticking out from different places and pushed my finger down inside the tiny pocket.

"I'll show you what those are for in in a moment, my dear. First, try on your coat." She helped me on with the coat, and it fit perfectly. "You are to try and remain unnoticed, of course, but if someone does happen to notice you, they will just think you some garish American airship cadet, That's all." She smiled and then winked at me. "And they would be half right."

I playfully swatted at her before turning my attention back to my gorgeous new coat. The inside had several pockets and loops. The outer edge looked as though it buttoned all the way down the front, but when I tried to button it, I noticed that they were on the wrong side and there were no button holes.

"It fastens like this." Fanny took the edges of the coat and overlapped them with the button side on top. Then she closed it with eye and hook fasteners spaced about every five inches reaching down to my thighs. "For quick removal," she said, and smiling did a quick motion with her hands and unfastened all of them at once.

"Now into your new corset." She helped me off with the coat and into the corset, which strangely was worn on the outside. Then without another word, she left the room. While waiting for her return, I regarded myself in the looking glass and, aside from the messy sleep hair, I did look considerably better than I had in the clothes from the previous night.

Fanny returned carrying the weapons kit she kept hidden beneath the floor boards. She took the stake out from under my pillow first and slipped it in the large loop on the left side of the corset. It was in the perfect position. I practiced by drawing it out a few times and replacing it. Ingenious, really.

Next she pulled five vials out of her kit. They were about the length of my thumb, and just about as wide. She placed one in each of the smaller loops along the bottom right side.

"Holy water," she said. "If you need a distraction just long enough to get away, this is your best bet. It will burn them, but it will really make them angry as well. So ensure you can get away after using one. Then there is this..."

She handed me what looked like a pocket watch. After clipping the chain to the top of my corset, she placed it in the little pocket on the right side.

"A pocket watch," I said, smiling. "Afraid I will forget the time?"

"This is no ordinary pocket watch, my dear. Actually, it is not a pocket watch at all. It is a compass that I have bewitched for added protection. As long as you have it on your person, you are impervious to magic done against you."

"Even yours?" I reminded myself of how she calmed me down yesterday.

"Alas, even mine." Her jovial face beamed with pride as she beheld me in my strange slaying outfit.

"So it works along with the amulet?"

"Yes. This will not only protect your mind, as the amulet does, but it will also protect your entire person from magical spells. And this special compass does not point north, my lamb. If a vampire is near, it will point toward the beast."

"You made it do that?"

"It is a special spell I have been working on. When your friend Conrad gave this to me to give to you, I thought it the perfect time to use it, since the compass was broken anyway."

"This is Conrad's compass?" A lump quickly grew in my throat, and I tried to keep from crying. I didn't succeed. Pulling the compass out of its little pocket, I looked for the inscription carved in the brass lid. It read, "To Find Your Way Back To Me." My tears blurred the words, so I wiped them away. The tarnished metal felt cold against my palm. It was nothing special, really, aside from the inscription. Just a plain, old compass, but I knew what it meant to Conrad. It was only thing he had left of his father. His mother had gifted it to his father during their last Christmas together. It was a rather expensive gift for the poor family, but they did have a lot of love between them.

His father died just a few weeks later.

Conrad had told me the heartbreaking story shortly after it happened, then he had never spoken of it again. His mother's mind had broken when she learned of her husband's accident at the factory. He had gotten caught up in the machinery and died from the loss of blood. She had heard the screams above the noise of the machines, for she had worked in the sewing room on the second level. Her supervisor had told all the women to keep working, that it was not of their concern. When she returned home that night, his affects were waiting for her along with an explanation. She sat in a chair and just stared at nothing for days on end. Echoes of his screams had kept her awake at night, so she was unable to sleep. She was unable to work or care for Conrad.

After they had fallen behind in their rent, the authorities had come for Conrad and his mother. When he had heard the pounding on the door, he had grabbed the compass and a pocket watch, as they had been laying out on the dresser, trying to hold onto anything from his father and the way life had been. Conrad had tried to hide in the closet behind some boxes. But once they came in, they found him and dragged him out of there. Conrad had been able to push the compass down into his pocket while in the closet, but the pocket watch had still been in his hands. They took it from him, saying something about how that would help because they were not get paid enough for having to deal with mad people.

Conrad was sent to the workhouse and his mother to the asylum. He had been able to keep the compass hidden and away until after he had escaped that awful place. Now, he always kept it close to him, next to his bed. Tarnished, but it was his nonetheless.

Now it was mine.

"Why are you crying, my dear?" Fanny asked.

"This was very special to Conrad. I cannot believe he gave it to me."

"You must be very special to him, my lamb."

I remembered how Conrad looked at me last night and now knew beyond any doubt that he loved me. He would not give me something so precious otherwise, but I didn't love him. I couldn't. He was my best friend in the world, but I just didn't love him in that way. Up until the night of my party, romance and marriage were the last things I wanted in my life, but then I saw Ashe. My heart changed so drastically in that one moment.

After placing the compass back in its little pocket, I wiped away my tears, trying not to think about how complicated things had become in just a few days.

"Are you all right, Nicole?" Fanny asked, concerned at my melancholy.

I covered by looking down at my bare feet on the hardwood floor and wiggled my toes. "Just rather chilled is all," I lied.

"Oh! I almost forgot!" She led me over to the poorly wrapped package on the bed. "This one is from the boys. "When Conrad told me what it was, I was so relieved, as I didn't know what I was going to do about your feet. You certainly couldn't wear those clunky boots with this outfit. It just would not be seemly."

It had been wrapped in crumpled up newspapers that had been somewhat flattened and tied with twine. Inside the box were a pair of black boots. They looked rather worn, but they were indeed women's boots. Fanny got a pair of dark stockings from my bureau, and I put them on before trying them on. They laced up to just over my ankle, and they fit quite well. I tried them out, walking around my chamber. The wooden heels tapped on the ground with every step.

Fanny had me step into the spats, then she laced them up the front. They reached up just high enough to cover the bottom of my new trousers.

"There, now you look like a proper airship cadet."
She beamed with pride. "Perhaps the spats can hold an
extra stake or two while out hunting," she added. "Now
for the finishing touch."

"There is more?" I asked incredulously. I had never
gotten so many gifts at once. It was all rather over-
whelming. But my face fell when I saw what Fanny held
in her hands.

"As I mentioned, you cannot be recognized, besides,
they complete the uniform." She held out the airship
goggles and bade me put them on.

"No," I protested. "I'm not wearing those things,
Fanny. You said I should not draw attention to myself."

"Indeed, I did, my lamb. But look at yourself. Your
face must be covered. What if you run into one of your
parents' many acquaintances?"

She had a point. At least no one would recognize me.
Even I didn't recognize myself as I looked in the mirror.
The round airship goggles rather limited my peripheral
vision, which might cause a problem.

"I shall braid your hair before you go out tonight,
that way you will not need to worry about it falling
from you cap." She moved me to the center of the room
and then stepped back. "So, give them a try."

"What?"

"Just be careful of the furniture," Fanny said, "and
give us a back kick."

"I beg your pardon?" Surely she was joking, but she just stood there waiting with her arms crossed. "Here? In my chamber?"

"Yes, Nicole, just be careful of the furniture."

"All right." I got in my prepared stance. With a quick turn I kicked my right leg out in a back kick and then turned around to face Fanny, who was very nearly hopping up and down and clapping her hands in glee.

"What is it, Fanny?"

"Do it again! Do it again!" she exclaimed. "Only this time, hold the kick. That's, keep your leg extended."

I did as she said and was shocked to see that the wooden heel of the boot had extended out two inches to a sharp point. I lowered my leg and stood on the heel again, but it didn't feel any longer than the other one. I sat down and looked at the bottom of the right boot. Upon closer inspection, I noticed that the sharpened heel was nestled up inside the basic heel of the boot. Then, there near the toe, was a button of sorts.

"How very curious."

"It is from your friend, Franklin," Fanny said.

I did the kick again, and the stake did exactly the same thing. It came out and then went back in as I stepped down on it.

"How did he do that?" I asked rhetorically.

"Don't ask me. You always told me that lad was a genius."

"No doubt," I responded, still marveling at my gadget. "Fascinating chap, that Franklin."

Chapter Eight

In Which Nickie Nick
Meets Some Zombies

Turns out Wilfred gave me a gift of his own as well. While I was out last night, he and Fanny were busy at work themselves. Fanny not only had Judith get me some larger corsets and day dresses for training, but she and Wilfred had made me my own secret weapons hideaway. Beneath the carpet in my bedchamber, they had cut out part of the floor boards and hinged it. All my new hunting clothes, my staking boots, and the weapons were hidden safely for no one to find. Just the three of us knew it was there.

All this without my parents knowing a thing.

It was all rather fun, this secret, vampire hunter identity.

Fanny led me in about an hour of training, picking up where we had left off yesterday. She commented on how quickly I was learning, but then, I was The Protector. It was all innate, it seemed. All the moves and kicks and such came to me as if I was remembering them rather than learning them. My body knew exactly what to do, and my mind was not far behind.

It was nearing two when my parents returned with their packages, so Fanny dressed me in a nice new skirt and blouse for the day. As I came downstairs, my parents were in the library, just adjacent to the foyer.

"Happy Christmas, Mother, Father."

Father turned around with his pipe clamped tightly between his teeth and looked over his newspaper at me. "Happy Christmas, my dear!" He dropped one side of the newspaper to open his arms, inviting me into an embrace.

"Have you been sneaking apple tarts again?" my mother sneered.

"No mother, I assure you." I sat on the settee next to her. She patted my skirts with a white gloved hand and turned back to her glass of wine.

"What did you find at the shops, mother?" I asked.

"Oh some very lovely things, indeed. I found a new hat. It is from Paris—all the rage there. I shall be wearing it tomorrow afternoon when our visitor comes."

"Visitor?" I asked.

"Of course, visitor. Are you daft, girl? Visitor! Have you forgotten? Lord Godwyn is coming to call on you tomorrow afternoon!"

I had forgotten, and I so wished the image of Lord Godwyn had stayed buried deep, for the thought of spending Christmas with that fop, listening to him prattle on, was not a pleasant one. No, I would much rather spend it out on the streets. Perhaps I could run into Ashe again. This time, dressed as a woman. Of course, mother would never approve, as he was likely an orphan at best or a chimney sweep at worst. But I didn't care. In fact, it may have made him that much more desirable. It was my life, after all.

"Have you a gift for Lord Godwyn?" my mother asked.

"No. Do I need a gift for him? He is the one calling on me."

"It is only proper! It is Christmas after all!"

I sat with my hands folded properly in my lap and looked at my mother blankly.

"Very well," she said. "Get your wrap. We are going to the shops. Benedict." She snapped her fingers to draw his attention away from the newspaper he had begun reading again. "Have Lucian bring the carriage around."

"We just got home, Greta. Give a man a break."

Father was speaking about himself, not Lucian.

"There will be time for lethargy after Christmas. Benedict. Now, please," my mother said in her softly demanding way.

Father closed his newspaper with a rustle and dropped it on the floor next to his comfy chair. The headlines read "Dozens of Factory Workers Missing" across the top of the paper. Down the side column was a picture of the Rickett Carriage I had seen last night, or at least, one very similar to it. The caption read "The Future is Here."

"Go get your wrap," my mother repeated, tearing me away from the newspaper.

"Is everything all right at the factory, mum?" I asked, indicating the headlines.

She sighed. She didn't care to talk about the business with me. She said it was not my concern, but I refused to move until she answered.

"There have been a few men gone missing, yes," she admitted.

"What do the police think?" I asked.

"That's neither my nor your concern, child. Go get your wrap." This time, the demand was not quite as soft, so I did as I was told.

"What do you think of this," my mother asked, holding up a pair of handsome leather gloves.

"Rather posh, Mother. And quite pricey, too." We were truly all right, financially, but there was no sense in being wasteful. Especially when others had so very little.

"This is *Lord* Godwyn, Nicole. *LORD* Godwyn. He is the most eligible bachelor in all of London for a family such as ours, and for some reason he has set his eyes on you. Let us keep it that way, shall we?"

"But Mother, he is a complete bore."

If we had not been in a public place, she likely would have slapped me for my cheek. Instead, she roughly grabbed my arm, smiled sweetly at the shopkeeper, and led me back outside into the cold, December air.

"How dare you embarrass me like that in public, young lady!" she huffed.

"Sorry, Mother. It shan't happen again. I still must not be feeling all that well," I said, knowing arguing with her was pointless.

"You are an ungrateful wretch, you are. There," she said, pointing across the street. "Your father is over there at the baker's. Go to him, and I shall buy something for Lord Godwyn from you."

"Very well, Mother," I mumbled and then added under my breath, "You should marry him, too."

"And no apple tarts for you," she added.

With a scowl, I started off across the street but was immediately overtaken by a group of marching men. They looked very similar in countenance as those from last night. The same blank stares paralyzed their faces. Their mouths were hanging slightly open, and they all marched in step with one another. I pulled back just in time from being run over by them.

"How very curious," I said aloud to myself.

Just past me on the sidewalk, other shoppers were not so lucky. The marching men ran straight into one woman, sending all her packages flying onto the cobblestones. Another couple were thrown back against the shop window.

"Now see here," I heard the man say, and his wife chimed in with a "I beg your pardon!"

"Nicole!" My mother rushed out of the shop. "Are you all right? Who were those men?"

"I don't know, Mum."

"The one looked very much like Mr. Whitewood from the factory, but he has not been to work in quite some time." She looked down the street after the marching men, annoyed. "Your father will not be pleased when he hears about this, and I'm afraid Mr. Whitewood will not have a job when he decides to return." She turned in a temper back into the store one last time, picked up her purchase, which was now wrapped in fanciful paper and tied in a red bow, grabbed my arm again and started off across the street to collect my father.

"Benedict! You will never guess who I just saw. Mr. Whitewood! He was walking along with that band of... thugs. Knocked that poor woman right into the street." She pointed her fur muff at the woman brushing snow from her skirts. Several well-dressed men had come to her aid, but the group of marching men had turned a corner somewhere and could no longer be seen.

"Is that so?" was all that father said. He puffed on his pipe and put the white bakery box under his arm. He signaled Lucian, who was waiting in our brougham just up the street, and the carriage came clattering down.

"Is that all you have to say, Benedict?" My mother's face was all flushed with the excitement.

A small group of street urchins who had been peering in the bakery window gathered at my father's feet.

"Please sir," the tallest one said. "We haven't eaten in days. Could you spare some bread? Or anything? Please?"

My heart went out to them. They couldn't have been older than Edwin, all small ones, likely sent to beg by their drunkard father, or worse, just living on the streets. It was such a common sight in London, but I never got used to it. Especially ones this young.

"Have you no manners?" my mother snapped at them just as the carriage pulled up.

"Lucian," my father said to the driver, ignoring mother and the young boys altogether, "take us to the factory."

"Yes, sir."

The young orphans bowed their head and moved back to the bakery window, dreaming of something to eat.

"Sorry," I offered, but before I could say more, my mother yanked me around and pushed me toward the carriage.

My father held my elbow as I stepped into the cab and then did the same for my mother before joining us inside.

I didn't say anything on the ride to the factory, and I tried to block out the rantings of my mother, first on the gall of those children and then on the gall of Mr. Whitewood. From the look on my father's face, so was he. Mother's life was quite good, so she truly should not complain. Still, she usually did.

We crossed Westminster Bridge, and I was quite happy to do so, as it was my favorite bridge in all of London. I was fortunate to be on the side of the carriage where I could see the Houses of Parliament on the way across, even luckier that the hour struck. The full, rich sounds of Big Ben filled the air and my mind, taking it off the hungry children momentarily. We could rarely hear the bells from our house, so it was truly a treat to hear them chime. The black waters of the Thames contrasted the banks, covered in snow and ice. The streets and tree limbs were also dusted in white. This year, a huge wreath was hung just beneath the east-, west-, and north-facing clock faces. Smaller wreaths decorated the gaslights along each side of the bridge. It all looked perfect set against the hazy grey-blue winter sky, with a fine mist hanging in the air. It was a truly magical time to be in London.

I watched the gaslights and holiday decorations reflecting in the Thames as we rattled along Victoria Embankment on the way to the factory. Mum prattled about business to father nearly the entire way there, but my mind was by then far away. Resting my cheek in my hand, I thought again of Ashe. Mad, really, that I was so taken with him. He could be anyone, and he was most certainly not of a station of which my parents would approve. He was likely an orphan like Conrad and Franklin and the others, but I didn't care. I just wanted to look into his dark eyes again.

Ashe had been so brave last night, fighting the vampire alongside me, although he had also been rather rude. Had it been any other man, I would have given him a what for, but I was most definitely stuck by this gentleman. And he might just be a gentleman, for he was dressed well enough. As for the soot, if anyone knew about dirt on the face it was me with all my nighttime adventures. Dirt and soot washes away. Perhaps it is a disguise of sorts as well.

When we arrived at the factory, one of the largest buildings in all of London, Father took my mother's hand, assisting her descent from the carriage, and then my own. The factory dominated a full city block and employed over two thousand workers.

Inside the eight-storey-high Hawthorn Textile Mill was a storm of sound and movement. We came in on the street level and stood on a long, wooden boardwalk that led to stairs going both up and down. The first four stories consisted of one room, starting at the cellar level. This was where the main manufacturing took place. On one side of the warehouse, huge steam-powered machines run by hundreds of workers wove thread into cloth. The arms of the weaving machines went to and fro, never missing a beat as if they were the tinny tempo of a grand march. Workers monitored the thread going into the machine, and had to detangle any tangles between the movement of the arms. Interlocking gears, each half the size of a man, spun along the edges of the imposing machine, all driven by a belt-powered steam engine. It was in one of those machines that Conrad's father got hurt. The other boys, too. Unfortunately, accidents like that were all too common, and it left orphans just like my band of boys. At least they had each other, and Conrad to look after them.

Big brass vats of colored, boiling water to dye the textiles lined the back wall. Workers stood over the vats with long wooden poles stirring the fabric to get an even dye throughout. Their clothes had been stained a mishmash of colors from the rising steam and the splashing water. From dye, the fabric then went into steam-powered driers, which took up the second half of this massive first story. The drying machines would not only dry the fabric, but also measure, cut, and wrap it into bolts for transport or sale.

A portion of the fabric stayed in house. The second part of the Hawthorn Textile Mill was upstairs, where hundreds of women sat at sewing machines making clothes. This is where Conrad's mother had worked. The specialty of this factory were short trousers, or knickers. But they also made shirts, skirts, and the like, mostly for the masses. For anyone of good birth or monied would have all their clothes tailor-made specifically for them.

It was easy for me to get new clothes for the boys when they needed it and to get boy's clothes for myself. Fanny, after being with the family for so long, got some special perquisites. One of those was getting clothes for her nephews and other family members when they needed something new, although she didn't actually have any nephews or living relatives. It was through this guise that we were able to help the boys and clothe me for my adventures without extra expense.

"Happy Chris'mas, Govna," a snaggle-toothed, leathery man said. This was Mr. Brock, father's factory manager. Mr. Brock looked rather like a weasel in a waistcoat. A downright creepy man, he was.

"Good Day, Mr. Brock. Update?" They were shouting to each other to be heard over the cacophony of clanking machines.

"A'course, sir." Mr. Brock stood a little straighter and tipped his hat to me and my mother. "Ladies," he said. He looked straight at me and smiled.

My stomach turned.

I gave a quick curtsey, and my mother just ignored him and looked out over the machinery.

"Nufink new t'report, Gov. Everyfinks workin' fine." He took his hat off and scratched his head for a moment before replacing it. "Oh. Mr. Jarry got caught up th'machine, few days back. But all's well. Just lost a few fingas, is all. Didn't stop work for long, and 'e's at 'ome recoverin'. A good Christmas 'e'll 'ave, m'lord. At least 'e's not workin' on Chris'mas Eve like the rest of us." He laughed and massaged his scraggly jaw, but my father didn't return the smile.

"His position filled yet?" father said. Nothing mattered to father but profits.

"Yeah. The very same day, Gov. Work is 'ard to come by these days, sir. So there's always more willin' t'work."

"Very well, Mr. Brock. Good work."

"Fank you, sir."

"Any word on Mr. Whitewood?"

"No sir. None whatsoevah. Strange that," Mr. Brock said. "Wif everone needin' work an'all. Why would someone just stop comin'?"

"That's a good question."

"Yes, sir. Fank you, sir." He tipped his hat.

"Anyone else go missing, Mr. Brock?"

"No, sir."

"And upstairs? All well there, ol' chap?"

"Yes, sir. Oh. Come to fink of it, Mrs. Fellmer went into labor last week. Made a mess of finks upstairs, but it was cleaned up fast enough. And yeah," Mr. Brock said before my father could ask, "'er position's been filled already, Gov."

"Good man." Father took out his pocket watch from its waistcoat pocket and opened it. He snapped it shut again and looked out over his workforce. "Let everyone off an hour early today, Mr. Brock. For Christmas."

"Oh! Fank you, sir. That's very generous of you, sir." He tipped his hat again.

"Carry on."

Father led us back out to the carriage.

CHAPTER NINE

IN WHICH NICKIE NICK IS MISSING A FRIEND

"Stay off the streets if you can." Fanny finished lacing me up in my new corset. She tied it off at the bottom and spun me around to tie on the mini bustle, the bottom of which extended to my mid-thigh. I already had on the boots and spats. The boots looked almost new with their spiffy shine. Fanny helped me on with my long coat, its inner pockets and loops now full of stakes, extra holy water, and even a knife. She had plaited my long hair in a single braid down my back.

I put on my cap and turned to leave.

"Wait," she said. "Take these."

I had been hoping she would forget.

"Yes. Just wear them on your head like this." She put them around my neck and then propped them up just over the bill of my cap. "Put them over your eyes if you are near people. You must not–"

"–be recognized," I finished for her. "Yes, as you have mentioned. Repeatedly."

I felt rather ridiculous in my new Protector ensemble, but it would facilitate movement in a fight. The lengthy coat did cover up the trousers and corset, at least. In fact, the way it hung in the back over the mini-bustle looked quite proper. So I looked mostly normal, albeit quite modern. It was not as if I had not gone without a skirt before, just never without a skirt dressed as a girl.

"Conrad came by before dusk, but you were still out with your parents. He gave me the address of where they are now staying, or rather, a place to meet him tonight near where they are staying. He wants to meet you beneath the Waterloo Bridge at seven. Best to travel underground as much as you can," she said. I could see that she had her own reservations about my appearance, likely similar to mine. Still, most people were so wrapped up with their own lives, they rarely noticed anything around them, especially back in the shadows.

"Don't fret, Fanny." I did my best to soothe her worry. "I shall stay out of the light. Plus, it is Christmas Eve, so everyone will either be doing last minute shopping or they will be pissed at a pub or holiday party."

"Nicole Knickerbocker Hawthorn!" Fanny's shocked whisper chastised me. "Ladies don't use such language."

"My apologies, Fanny. I shall be more proper." I curtsied, which certainly must have appeared comical in my vampire fighting outfit because Fanny giggled.

"Silly girl," she said. "Now off with you."

"Aye-aye." I snapped to attention and saluted, fingertips touching my goggles.

Once out into the night, I moved quickly through the streets, keeping to the shadows. My movement was much more agile tonight, and I didn't know if it was my new powers settling into my limbs or the sleekness of my new garments. Perhaps a bit of both.

When I reached the banks of the Thames, I could see the dome of St. Paul's on the horizon over on north side. It glowed warmly in the cold night. Mass likely had already started.

Directly across the river from where I stood, the Egyptian Obelisk reached skyward. It had only been erected a few years back. My father brought me down to this very spot, to watch from across the river. There had been two monstrous scaffolds built out of wood. I remember watching for what seemed like a very long time, but little happened. I must have been about Rufus's age then. Father told me it took nearly a fortnight to raise it and set it in place properly.

I jumped off the side walls down onto the banks below. My heels sank in the soft mud, and I wondered how that would affect the staking mechanism within. I would have to talk with Franklin about that.

"Conrad?" I whispered, but there was no answer. I walked, mostly on my toes, toward the underside of the bridge. "Conrad?" I said again, but I heard nothing but the water licking the shore. It smelled quite odious down here, and I was glad I didn't have to scavenge around like Conrad and Rufus sometimes did for things to sell. What a horrible way to make a living.

"Conrad?" I tried one more time, raising my voice to just above a whisper.

"Well if it ain't Nick." A familiar voice came out of the darkness. "You are rather kitted up today, Nick." Ashe moved from beneath the bridge and looked at me with his head tilted slightly, as if he was trying to figure something out.

"Ashe." I felt my face flush. Good thing we were in the mostly dark. "What are you doing here?"

"Conrad asked if I would wait and bring you to him and the others. Something's happened today. Follow me," he said, and I did. I walked directly behind him, literally in his footsteps, and he led me into one of the sewer's openings. I thought the banks of the Thames had smelled bad, but this, in the brick enclosed space, was even worse. Fortunately, the water was very low. It didn't even reach the lower edge of my spats. The bottom rim of my coat skimmed the surface.

"So," he began as we walked, slowing down and moving aside so that I would walk beside him. "What's with the togs? Taking a trip on an airship, are we? Or are you joining the RAN?" He indicated the airship goggles perched on my head.

"For fighting." My voice was a mixture of anger and embarrassment. "Fighting vampires."

"Is that right? Are you a professional vampire hunter now?" There was laughter in his voice. I wanted to hide and slap him all at the same time.

"More or less," I said indignantly. "What about you?"

"More or less," he echoed. "I guess we will be working together then."

The anger faded and a rush of joy quickly took its place, knowing I was going to see him again and often. A group of rats scuttled by and I couldn't contain a very girlie squeal as they ran over my shoes.

Ashe laughed. "Fearless, aren't you?"

"I will have you know that I'm more fit for this task than you are." The anger had come back and brought a friend. He turned and pinned me against the wall faster than I could even see. He hovered over me, my back against the curved brick wall. Next to my head, his arm braced him as he bent in close to me. His lips were just inches from mine. The excited nausea returned and I held my breath waiting for what I hoped would come next.

"Don't be so sure of that, Nick," he whispered. The nearness of his lips to mine heated my cheeks. His dark eyes bore into mine, and his scent, a mixture of musk and cinnamon, intoxicated me and drowned my reason. In that moment, I was completely his.

Then, without another word, he pushed himself away and continued walking.

As soon as I had caught my breath, I followed in his footsteps once more.

"You didn't fool me last night, you understand." He stayed ahead of me this time.

"What?" I eloquently responded.

"Dressed as a boy. I knew you were no lad."

"Y–you didn't," I sputtered. "How?"

"You smelled of heather. No street urchin I've ever met smelled of heather." There was that laughter in his voice again. He was enjoying this.

My father got our soap imported from Scotland, and it was scented with heather. How could he know that? How could he *smell* that?

"Have you been fighting vampires long?" I asked, trying to change the subject, but my mind stayed on how he knew. He had been at my party, too, albeit outside. Surely the two were no coincidence, but now was not the time to ask.

"About six months," he responded. "Didn't even know they existed before that. Now I kill as many as I can." His voice had turned into a growl near the end. "So, what's your story? Why do you fight them?"

"I'm not supposed to tell." Pathetic. Why did everything I say to this man sound so very childish?

"Will daddy spank you?" He mocked me.

"No," I snapped. "If you must know"–and he might as well know if we would be hunting together. It would explain my attire anyway–"I'm The Protector."

No sooner were the words out of my mouth than he stopped short, causing me to run into the back of him. He turned, and he was once again but inches from me.

"The Protector?" He loomed over me, and I felt his eyes searching for the truth.

"Y–yes," I choked.

"You. You're *The* Protector?"

"Yes. I'm *The Protector*." Annoyed now. Why was that so hard for him to believe?

"You fulfilled the Hawthorn Legacy?" His eyes still searched my face for something. He took a step closer.

My metal, lace collar felt rather tight. I swallowed hard. "How did you know about that?"

"Nevermind. Are you a Hawthorn?"

"Yes. My name is Nicole Knickerbocker Hawthorn," I said proudly. "All this Legacy stuff just happened a few days ago on my seventeenth birthday. It was all rather sudden."

"Nicole Knickerbocker." He smiled, more relaxed now. "Nickie Nick."

"Don't call me that," I spat, gritting my teeth.

He laughed, then turned and began walking again. "I knew I had felt something that night," he mumbled to himself.

"What did you say," I asked. Was he referring to the night of my party?

But he ignored my question, and now it was he who changed the subject. "It's just up here." He pointed to a wrought iron ladder leading up to street level.

I couldn't say I was sorry to leave the sewers.

"Ladies first," he said with an exaggerated bow.

The metal rungs felt hard and cold, even through my gloves. I started to climb the ladder, and he came right behind me. When we reached topside, I had no idea where we were. It was dark, and we were definitely in an alley. Two dark buildings stretched up on either side of us. Although I was very happy to be out of the sewers, this place looked fairly dodgy.

"Where are we?" I asked.

"Near Blackfriars." He lowered the iron sewer cover back into the street. "It's just through here."

I followed him down the alley and through an old wooden door near the back of the building to our right. Once inside, there was a door to the left and a staircase that went straight up to the second story, and to the subsequent floors above that, but we just went up one flight. Taking one of the keys hanging from a large ring that dangled from a chain attached to his waistcoat, he opened the door.

"Is this your place?" I asked.

"I don't live here, if that's what you mean," he answered.

Cut the cryptic, I wanted to say, but I held my tongue. Must have been all those years of training to be a lady of society. I followed him inside, and he closed and locked the door behind me. Now a wholly disturbing thought came to mind. How could I know I could trust him? I just went into a strange place with a man I had only met once. Although I was undeniably drawn to him, I didn't know him at all. My body tensed at the possible danger, as I would not be ruined without a fight, and I didn't like the man's odds going up against my strength and speed.

He moved past me and said, "I have brought your friend."

Conrad appeared a moment later in the entryway. "Hey Nick, come in." He didn't smile, as he usually did when he saw me, and he looked rather pale and sickly.

I followed him into a rather nice room, considering they had just been living in an abandoned cellar. This room had a few pieces of furniture and a fireplace as well. There was even a fire in the fireplace, which was a luxury these boys had not often had.

"Conrad. Is this your new place? Wherever did you find it?"

"Mr. Tanner here," he said, indicating Ashe.

"Mr. Tanner?" I asked.

"Ashe Tanner, at your service, Miss." Ashe gave a real formal bow this time. "It belonged to a colleague of mine," he explained, "but he is no longer in any shape to utilize it. I was very glad to have run into Mr. Hannon today."

"Yeah. This was much better than the place I had found. Which was really just an offshoot of a sewer line. Not great."

"Where are the others?" I asked, looking around.

"Edwin's asleep in the bedroom and Franklin is in the kitchen, working. He's already set up quite the workshop in there for himself. Mr. Tanner says no one will bother us here. Still," Conrad said. "I wish we had found it before low tide today." His face fell. Actually, saying that isn't quite accurate. Conrad had not seemed very happy about his new place, and he should be ecstatic at Mr. Tanner's generosity. He had given a half-hearted smile once or twice when talking about the flat, but now I realized he was not happy at all. Distracted. Then I remembered Ashe saying that something had happened.

"What happened, Conrad? Where's Rufus."

"That's just it, y'see? He's gone."

"The traps?" I asked. With their habit of stealing for food and other necessities, the police were a constant threat to their freedom.

"Not the traps," he continued. "We was down by the river, collecting bits of things to sell, as we do. We was working two parts, but I always kept him in my sight. Always. Next thing I knew. A man was with him on the bank. I shouted at him and the man, but it was as if Rufus didn't hear me. The man looked up, so I know he should've, but Rufus, he didn't look over at me or nothin'. I ran along the bank to get to him, but the man had picked him up and carried him away. I was shoutin' the whole way, but I couldn't catch up. It was like everything was covered in a thick fog for a minute and then, when it cleared, they were gone."

"How very curious," I said. "Did you see anything else? What about the man? Did you recognize him?"

"Nope. Never seen him before, but he was wearing somethin' strange. Some sort of machine over one shoulder."

CHAPTER TEN

IN WHICH NICKIE NICK VISITS TRAFALGAR SQUARE

I rushed downstairs into the dark alley, and Ashe followed closely behind.

"Where do we begin, Mr. Tanner? London is a very big city, and he could be almost anywhere by now." I wrung my hands and paced to and fro.

"We shall find him, Nickie. Don't fret."

"Don't fret? He's like a little brother to me. They all are, and I cannot bear to think what might be happening to him." I buried my face in my hands and tried not to cry, but the tears came. The horror stories of children kidnapped and forced to work in such horrible and wretched ways filled my thoughts, and I couldn't push them away. In my own darkness, I felt an arm settle around my shoulders. Ashe pulled me close to him, comforting me.

"We shall find him" he repeated.

"What's the use of all these new abilities if I cannot protect the ones I love? The Protector, indeed."

Although I was very worried about Rufus, I really felt strangely safe in Ashe's arms. But a moment later he pushed me away from him, held me by the shoulders, and looked me straight in the eyes. I blinked the tears away and looked up at him, expectantly.

"Standing here weeping about it will not find him," he said gently, but the words were harsh. And true. I wiped my cheeks dry and strode out into the street. The cold winter air stung my tear-stained cheeks, but I was determined to find my friend.

"You are right, of course, Mr. Tanner. We shall start where he was taken, down by the river." Without waiting to see if Ashe was behind me, I headed out along the street. Any previous insecurity about my abilities or even my outfit washed away and was replaced with determination. I would find Rufus, and he would be safe. "If any vampire gets in my way tonight, he is dust," I informed the night.

The tide was up, so I was unable to jump down onto the shore as before. Taking a deep breath, I tried to focus inward. Tap into my power or senses or something. There was that feeling again, the one I had had before when a vampire was around, but it was very faint. I spun around, but the only person approaching was Ashe.

"Are you Nickie Nick?" a small voice peeped in the shadows.

"Who's there?" I asked.

"It's just me. Cassie," the small voice spoke again. "My dolly told me to come here to meet you. She said you could help." A young girl came out of the darkness into the nearby gaslight. Just another orphan on the streets. She couldn't have been more than six years old, and she was hugging a broken china doll close to her chest. Its pale porcelain face was rather horrifying, cracked with missing chunks. It had blonde ringlets for hair, and its pale blue dress was torn and dirtied. One blue eye stared out into nothing. The other was completely missing, leaving a gaping, jagged hole in its place. The cracks from the missing eye extended up into its hairline and down its nose. Its lips were somehow too red.

"What are you doing out here, little girl? This is no place for you. It's dangerous here."

"My name is Cassie," she said defiantly. "And I told you, my dolly told me to come meet you. It is very important. You can help the boy."

"The boy? Do you know about Rufus? Did you see him taken today?"

"No." Her little brow furrowed. "I told you, my dolly told me! Are you listening to me?" She stamped her little foot and put her hands on her hips. She held onto the doll with its one remaining arm, and it lolled by her side in a most disturbing way.

Cassie herself was very dirty, as if she had been living on the streets for quite some time, and she was thin, but not deathly so. Her brown hair was pulled to the sides in two ratty pigtails, and her dress was stained. The hem was torn as well.

"Mr. Tanner." I turned to Ashe. It did feel strange calling him Mr. Tanner since I had met him as Ashe and I felt so oddly close to him already, but such were the rules of society. "Please take this child back to the flat. Conrad will look after her until we are done."

"I'm not leaving you out here alone, *Miss Hawthorn*," he sneered.

"You're not listening to me," Cassie said again, this time rather loudly. "Why don't no one listen to me?"

"I'm listening," I answered, trying to appease the child. No sense in her calling attention to us all out here in the darkness near a fairly dodgy area. "What do you know about the boy? What did your dolly tell you?"

"He's with a very bad man."

I gasped and brought my hand up to my mouth, shocked. All those horrid thoughts came rushing back.

"He's not hurt, though. Not really. It's like he's sleeping. Awake, but sleeping," Cassie continued. She looked up at Ashe and then back down at me.

"Did your dolly tell you where he is with this bad man?"

"No, miss. I just get pictures in my head sometimes. Like dreams, only I'm awake."

"And have you seen any pictures about this boy and this bad man?" I asked. Why was I listening to this little girl and her stories? Surely this was all balderdash, but something deep inside me said to listen. Perhaps she did know something. After all, I was The Protector and my governess a witch. The past few days had certainly readjusted my notion of reality. Besides, how else would she have known my name?

"Yes. Four lions around a very tall tower."

"Trafalgar Square," Ashe said without hesitation. He was right, she was talking about Trafalgar Square.

"Get her back to the flat, Mr. Tanner." I took the girl's doll-free hand and stood up to face Ashe. "I shall head over to Trafalgar."

"You are not going alone." He stepped closer to me, blocking my path.

"Yes, I am, Mr. Tanner," I replied sternly. "I'm The Protector. It is my duty."

"I'm coming with you."

"Fine," I replied, handing the child's hand over to Ashe's. "Get her inside and warm. Have Conrad feed her, then meet me at Trafalgar Square."

I didn't stick around for a reply, but rather turned and ran quickly away, pulling the goggles over my eyes as I mounted the bridge full of people. My coat flapped behind me as a ran, but I didn't care that my trousered legs were exposed as I ran across Waterloo Bridge. Once on the other side, I ducked back into the shadows and stayed off the main roads until I reached Trafalgar Square, and it was bustling with movement on this Christmas Eve evening.

"Now what?" I asked the night and lifted the goggles back to my hat.

"He's a teacher," Ashe's voice came from behind me, and I spun around to face him.

"How did you get here so fast?" I asked. He was not even out of breath.

"Cassie said that her doll told her that the bad man was a teacher, too."

"A teacher, like a professor perhaps? I guess That's as good a place as any to start," I said. "Take that side of the street, and I'll take this side."

"Do you believe her, Nick? I mean, she is an orphaned child rambling nonsense, likely mad as well." Ashe didn't move to the other side of the street, but rather stayed very, very close to me as I began searching the door plates.

"I don't know if I believe her, Mr. Tanner."

"Enough of this Mr. Tanner, all right?" He stopped me, and his intense eyes caught mine, chasing all thought out of my head. He held me by the shoulders as he lectured. "Just call me Ashe. I certainly don't stand on ceremony. This is not High Society, Nick. We are on the streets, so can we just leave the pretension behind?"

"Certainly," I whispered, blushing and looking down at my feet. My heart pounded, but I took a deep breath and turned from him, pressing on and looking door to door until I saw or felt something. I wasn't even sure what I was looking for, or waiting for.

Just trust the process, I told myself. Something would most certainly have to turn up.

A man stepped out from the shadows and pointed a copper-colored gun at us. "Wallet," he grunted. Grabbing my arm, he shoved the gun into my ribs and dragged me into the alley.

Ashe followed, and his face turned almost feral with anger.

"Let her go," Ashe growled.

"Or what, Gov'na? You gonna hurt me, pretty boy?" The gruff man stuck the gun deeper into my side.

"Let her go!" Ashe took a step toward the man, but the robber didn't hesitate. He turned the gun on Ashe and shot.

Ashe reeled backward and fell onto a pile of boxes before hitting the cobblestones with a loud, wet thud.

"No!" I screamed and smelled the blood, but the man just held me more tightly.

Instinct kicked in, too late for Ashe's sake, but I turned and knocked the gun from the now-surprised man's hand and clocked him with a right across the jaw. The man stumbled back but regained his balance quickly, coming at me swinging. I blocked a punch and threw another back at him, followed by a kick to the chest. Lucky for the man, it was not with the stake boot. The robber hit the side of the building, his head whipping back against the bricks. After a sickening crack, the man crumpled into a heap, coloring the snow red.

Ashe lay motionless on the street, and the snow around him was red as well. The bullet had entered his stomach. I rushed to his side to see how much damage was done.

"Ashe? Oh my goodness. Ashe? Can you hear me?" I brushed his dark hair off that beautiful face. His lips were slightly parted and quite crimson in color. "Ashe?"

He didn't move. The wet, red snow framed his fallen form, and I shook him again.

"Ashe!" The tears came. "No, Ashe. Please. Not after I just found you."

I put my ear against his chest, but I didn't hear a heartbeat.

"Oh my goodness! Ashe!" I shook him again and cried. "Please, no. Not like this. I've just found you, my sweet love. Please!"

He stirred.

"Oh, thank the heavens! Ashe, you'll be all right," I wiped the tears from my eyes so that I could see him clearly and started to get up. I had to act quickly. "I'll get you to a hospital, and you'll be all right."

He sat up and grabbed my arm, keeping me from standing, and just looked at me. The snow had washed away the soot on one side of his face, and through the smeared blackness showed pale skin. More pale than was fashionable, deathly white. Upon a closer look, tiny blue veins webbed out from around the edges. Then he did something altogether unexpected. Opening his shirt, he exposed flesh even whiter than his cheek. He thrust a finger in the bullet hole and pulled out the offending metal with a gasp. Almost immediately afterward the wound began to close.

I pulled out of his grasp, stood up, and backed away from him with eyes wide.

"I guess I should have told you right off," Ashe said, not looking directly into my eyes but rather off to the side as if he was embarrassed. "It happened about six months ago, and I hate it. I hate myself for what I am. That's why I kill them, Nickie. That's why I vowed to destroy them, because they made me into this."

His eyes found mine across that dark alley, searching for acceptance.

"You are a...." I couldn't bring myself to say it.

"Yes, a vampire," he finished for me, looking away again. "I don't kill people, though. I'm no danger to you or to any human. I'm on your side in this fight. Do you trust me?"

What could I say? Did I trust him? He had in essence lied to me, although it was clear as to why.

Still. A vampire.

I couldn't deal with this now, so I didn't say anything and just went back to the task at hand. Leaving Ashe and the fallen robber in the alley, I turned back onto the street and searched. From door-to-door I searched, checking the names on the doors. On the plaques. Checking the shops.

Ashe walked just behind me.

"Nickie," he said, but I didn't respond.

I didn't know what to say to him, so I said nothing.

"Nicole." He broke the silence between us with his stern tone, stopping me and spinning me around to face him. My hand went for the stake in my corset, but his hand stopped mine from drawing it. "I'm not going to hurt you, Nicole. This does not change anything."

"This changes everything, Ashe!"

"How does this change anything? I'm still helping you find your friend. I fought with you against the monsters yesterday, and I shall continue fighting and killing vampires. Had that robber been a vampire and not human, I would have moved much faster. Like I said, I don't hurt humans. I may no longer be one, but I retain my humanity by choice."

His eyes pleaded with me and his jaw was tense awaiting my reply. We stood there on Whitehall, and it began to snow. I watched the tiny flakes hit his beautiful face, and I wanted to cry.

He was my enemy.

He was what I was destined to kill, yet my heart reached out to his, ached for him. My soul called out for him, and there was no denying that.

Behind me in the distance, Big Ben chimed. I turned to see the great clock tower peeking up over the treetops, and I counted.

Eight o'clock.

A tear spilled over my lid and I angrily wiped it away.

"Let's go," I said to Ashe. "No time for this now. Rufus needs us."

That seemed good enough for him, as he came without a word.

Chapter Eleven

In Which Nickie Nick
Sees Rufus

Ashe's eyes bore into the back of my skull as we made our way down Whitehall until we could no longer see the spindle. I crossed over and came back up the east side of Whitehall, but we came up with nothing. Most doors had nothing on them, and the few that did, we saw no sign of a school or a professor or anything. There was not much I could do about Ashe being a vampire at the moment, as I truly needed his help to find Rufus. Not really knowing if I could trust him, for we only had just met, I kept a stake gripped tightly in my right hand. No doubt he noticed, for when we reached Trafalgar Square again, he came up next to me and the look on his face was one of a wounded heart, which made mine soften to him once again. I slipped the stake back in its loop on my corset and looked an apology at him. After all, he had not chosen this life, no more than I had chosen to be the daughter of heartless industrialists or The Protector. I did welcome the birthright, however. Perhaps I could save more people than my parents had hurt. Tip the scales to good.

Something caught my eye across the square, on the far side. It was a group of marching men. Four across and at least ten deep. They all moved in step with the same blank stares as the ones I had seen earlier in the day and yesterday as well, but there were many more of them here.

"Look there," I said to Ashe. "Does that seem odd to you?"

"Quite," he responded.

The men were not dressed in any sort of uniform. In fact, they were all wearing the ratty clothes of the working class and the poor.

"Come on." Ashe and I crossed the street over to the square. The group of men were coming around the spire. As they became visible again on our side of the lions, I saw, along the front of the squad, four shorter people. Children!

I ran past the horse statue toward the block of men, and sure enough, one of those short people was Rufus!

"Rufus!" I shouted, running towards them. "Rufus!" But he didn't look over at me. Neither did any of the other men. Other passersby stared at me shouting in the gaslit square on Christmas Eve, but none of the marching men even so much as flinched. They all wore the same blank expression on their faces, unblinking and staring straight ahead. When they finally blinked, it was all in unison.

Ashe pulled me back into him, and held me tight. I struggled to get away, but he whispered into my ear, "Not yet. We'll follow them. Something's not quite right. They appear to be under some sort of spell."

"No, Ashe. Let me go! Rufus!" I shouted again and struggled against Ashe, but even my Protector strength was no match for his. People were beginning to stare.

Ashe spun me around and pulled me into him, then, leaning down, covered my mouth with his cinnamon-colored lips. A rush of excitement flowed through me as he kissed me, and his lips were soft. Amazingly soft.

I forgot everything for that moment.

I forgot who I was.

I forgot about the marching men.

I forgot he was a vampire.

I forgot everything but his lips.

Then he pulled away but not very far. He held me there, just inches away, my lips still wet with his, and he whispered, "Not now, Nickie. We will save Rufus, but we must first figure out what is happening."

I nodded, unable to form words. After the men marched across the street and down Whitehall, Ashe released me and turned to follow them. I was unsteady on my feet and it took me more than just a moment to recover. When I did, I rushed up to Ashe, who was already across the street.

"What was that?" I said angrily.

"What?"

"You know what!" I was even angrier now that he was acting so nonchalant.

"Oh. The kiss? I had to do something to quiet you down," he said, grinning.

"That was completely improper, Mr. Tanner." I wanted him so desperately to kiss me again at the same time. "Do you have no manners, sir?"

His smile faded.

"Let's just see where these men are going, all right?"

I shoved my hands in my coat pockets to avoid smacking him.

To quiet me down. How infuriating! Indeed.

We followed the marching block of men for a good long while from a safe distance, but we never let them out of our sight. Down past the Houses of Parliament and across Westminster Bridge into South London they marched in unison, never missing a step.

Ashe and I had not said a word to each other in that entire time.

I had forgotten to pull the goggles back over my eyes, and there were people all around. Then someone caught my eye. There, just ahead and directly in our path, was Lord Godwyn. I pulled the goggles down quickly, just before his eyes fell on me. He had a woman on each arm, so his eyes were not on me for long. He passed by without a second look, as I looked nothing like the Nicole Hawthorn he knew.

Still. That was close.

His companions giggled, apparently at something His Most Annoying had said, which just confirmed their daftness. Reginald was never amusing, just tedious and tiresome. Now I wished to marry him even less than before, if that was possible.

Just as the marching men rounded the corner up ahead onto Borough Road, two obvious vampires accosted us from an alley.

"Well, if it ain't Mr. Tanner and his latest trollop," the older one said. I could tell he was older because he looked the least human. His fangs were long. Even with his mouth closed, they stuck out of his sneering mouth. His eyes were quite sunken, not just dark like Ashe's, but truly sunken back into his skull. His skin was pure white, and much thinner than Ashe's with many more veins showing, too. Even his ears looked pointed and abnormally long.

"Yeah, his trollop." The other one looked squarely at me, licking his lips and smacking as if sitting before a succulent meal, which, I guess to him, I was.

"I really cannot do this now, William."

"Oh, sorry about that, Mr. Tanner. Perhaps we can make an appointment to meet at a more convenient time. Got your diary handy, do ya?" He took a step closer, and Ashe took a step back, putting a protective hand up in front of me. I slapped it away, sick of his superior act. "Fiesty one you've got there." The older vampire's eyes flicked to me before settling back on Ashe.

"Do you want to see just how feisty," I said, setting into fighting stance.

"Tsk tsk tsk." The old vampire wagged his finger with a disgustingly long fingernail at me. "Quiet, girl. This is between me and Mr. Tanner, here."

"Let her go," Ashe repeated. "Like you said, it's between you and me. Just let her go. This doesn't concern her."

"No, William. I want her. I'm rather peckish." The younger one still appeared more human, but he was a revolting human at that. Missing teeth between his elongated canines and a bloated tongue that darted in and out of his drooling mouth, licking his lips and few remaining teeth.

I repressed a shudder. "I'm not going anywhere."

"Nick," Ashe said, warningly, but the drooling vampire came at me, so I spun around and kicked back as he lunged. I knew the muck from the Thames shore hadn't clogged up the works when my boot activated. By the time I had regained my fighting stance, all that was left of that lascivious creature was a pile of dust in the snow. Both the older vampire and Ashe stared at me with wide eyes and mouths gaping.

"Did I mention that I can take care of myself?" I huffed at them both, and then continued speaking to the old, sunken-eyed vampire: "Your turn, beautiful." I pulled the stake out of my corset and stood at the ready. After a quick look to Ashe and back at me, the old vampire turned and ran away, and I ran right after him. I spun him around and jammed the stake towards his heart, but he blocked it, knocking it out of my hand.

Hissing, he lunged toward my neck. When his teeth clanked against the metal collar, it distracted him for a moment. I took the opportunity to smash one of the holy water vials against his hardened cheek. He howled in pain and reared back ready to strike again, but I had already taken a second stake from an inside pocket and positioned it just right. The old vampire rushed right into the stake, but he realized his mistake at the last moment and pulled back. The stake entered his chest, but it didn't go deep enough to hit his heart. He looked down at the stake sticking out of his chest awkwardly, and before he could recover, I lunged forward with a flat palm strike, driving it home.

Dust.

I found the whoosh sound that came just as the vampire went from solid to dust oddly satisfying.

"Did you see which way they went?" I asked, turning back to face Ashe.

He blinked at me and closed his mouth. He composed himself once again. "Now I understand why you knocked my arm away. You don't need my protection, do you?"

"Like I said."

"They went to the left," he answered.

"Let's go," I ordered, already heading up the street and turning left, but as soon as I turned the corner, I stopped.

They were nowhere to be seen.

Ashe stopped beside me, and we both stood there silently.

I closed my eyes and tried to listen, but there was no sound of synchronized marching anywhere that I could hear.

"Hear anything?" I asked Ashe.

"Nothing other than normal night sounds," he said.

"We had not been detained for too long, so they couldn't have made it all the way up Borough, which means they either turned off the street or stopped somewhere along this road."

Although, as I looked around at the scores of possibilities, I didn't know where to begin.

CHAPTER TWELVE

IN WHICH NICKIE NICK
SITS IN THE SNOW

Midnight had struck, and the fading echoes of Big Ben's chimes haunted my soul. It was Christmas Day, and we were no closer to finding Rufus or the mysterious band of marching men.

"This is futile," Ashe said to me. "They could be anywhere, and not just around here. Or we might have already passed them. I mean, honestly, Nickie, what exactly are we looking for?"

Failure washed over me, and I sat down hard on the snowy curb. My nose had gone numb quite some time ago, and I could also no longer feel my toes. It snowed on and off all night, and although my constant movement kept my blood flowing, the temperature was dropping. I looked at my hazy shadow made by the gaslamp on the corner and felt the damp creep through my coat and trousers.

"I'm sure I don't know. Rufus. A clue. A lead of some sort. Perhaps I am just hoping to get lucky, but what I do know is that I cannot just leave him out there. He's like a little brother to me, Ashe. They are my family. The family I chose, not the family I'm stuck with." My teeth began to chatter and my body began to shiver.

Ashe sat down next to me, pulled his coat over my shoulders, and held me close, which certainly started to warm me up almost immediately.

Here I was in the early morning of Christmas Day being comforted by a vampire. How drastically my life had changed in the past few days. Like my grandfather used to say, 'You never know what's going to happen when you wake up in the morning.'

He had died when I was twelve, but I still remembered him well. Dead and gone forever, yet here was Ashe. Dead, as I understood it to work, but not gone.

"How did it happen?" I asked, looking up at him. His gaze was one of care and perhaps a little admiration. Could I let myself believe love? But once he realized what I was asking, he withdrew and his eyes went dark. Although his arm and coat still surrounded me, keeping my warmth in, I felt him pull away. It was most obviously a sensitive subject, but it was all so curious to me. I didn't press the issue but rather just waited until he was ready to answer, leaving the question hanging in the air like the fog around us.

We sat in silence for a long time, and just when I thought he would never answer, he spoke up. "About seven months ago," he began. "I came to London. My father is a tanner up in Yorkshire, and I had been learning the trade since I was a boy. But, I wanted more. I had heard stories of the city, and I thought I could make my own way here. I didn't want to turn into my father with skin as leathery as the hides with which he worked. The smell of lime and dung permeating everything. So, on my eighteenth birthday, I set out for London. I wanted to be more. Behold," he finished with his arms wide.

No hint of joy shone in his eyes. Only pain. Disappointment. Failure.

"You were attacked?"

"I was only here about a month, and I was hungry. Homeless. There was no work. I spent a night or two in a workhouse breaking rocks, and I realized what a good life a tanner had. The city was not what I had expected, and my thoughts more and more strayed to going back home and begging my father's forgiveness. He had said that I could never return, but since I was reduced to begging in London for food, it would be a step up to beg from my father.

"Then she came." His eyes became darker still. "She was the most beautiful woman I had ever seen. Fine dress. Fine jewels. I watched her walk by, and she looked over at me watching her and smiled. Then I saw them. Her fangs. At first I thought it was some strange hallucination from the hunger, but then she approached me and said she saw something in me, my strong features. Strength of character, she said, but how could she see that? I don't know. Perhaps she was just hungry herself. Perhaps it was just a game for her. She told me that she could make it so that I would never need food again. And I was so hungry and broken and foolishly idealistic, that I thought this was God sending me an angel to save me. For in all that time, no matter how hungry I got, I never stole even so much as a morsel of bread. For I was not blind. I could see all around me there were many in a worse way than me. Some diseased. Crippled. Children without anyone, forced to work in workhouses or worse, especially for the girls. After all, it had been my decision to come here. I deserved it for not appreciating what I had, for my greed in wanting more."

He shook his head and his eyes filled with blood tears. Although this shocked me, I couldn't help but feel for Ashe.

"Of course, I didn't know what she had meant, but I was so very desperate and she had been so beautiful, a symbol of what I thought was possible for me if just given the chance. Foolish, I was. She pressed her will onto me, the way only a vampire can, without words or physical force, just with her eyes. With her mind. And I relented. I let her drink me, nearly dry, turned out. Then she fed me her blood. I died after all. Everything went black, as if a dreamless sleep, but then I awoke once again, changed. Forever changed."

Ashe was quiet for a long moment, staring out into the darkness.

"I never saw her again. Pointless. It had all been so random and pointless. Wrong place, I suppose."

He got up from my side, leaving his coat around my shoulders.

"Ashe, your coat," I said. "You'll be cold."

"Don't you see, Nick? I'm always cold and I'm never cold. I'm always hungry and never hungry. I cannot feel anything." His eyes became soft again. He stooped down in front of me sitting there on the curb, my trousers now soaked through with melted snow, and took my hands into his. "Except when I'm with you, Nicole. Then I feel warm. Then I feel alive. From the moment I saw you through your window, I knew you were my salvation."

I swallowed hard and tried to look away from the intensity in his eyes. Forever was there, desperately trying to reach out to me. But I couldn't look away. I ached for him. The distraction kiss from hours back came back to me and I longed to taste his lips again. To feel his touch.

He leaned in, and I caught my breath.

"Well, Nickie Nick," Conrad's voice interrupted us. "I see you're doing your very best to find Rufus."

His face was a mixture of jealousy and rage. With his arms crossed, he glared down at me and Ashe. Behind Conrad stood Franklin, Edwin, and Cassie holding onto her broken doll.

"What are you doing down here?" I demanded, standing up a little too quickly, letting Ashe's coat fall onto the sidewalk. Ashe caught me as a stumbled toward him, which just made Conrad all the more angry. "This is no place for children, Conrad. You should know better." My embarrassment now mixed with anger at Conrad for placing the rest of them in danger, I stood facing Conrad with my hands on my hips, spreading my coat so that my knickers and spats showed.

"Nice outfit," Conrad spat.

Ashe moved behind me, as if to back me up if needed, but he knew this was between me and Conrad.

"We're here because Cassie wouldn't keep quiet," Conrad continued after a scowl at Ashe. "She has been demanding for hours that she knows more, that her dolly is talking to her. What's with all this, Nick?" Conrad moved a little closer to me and lowered his voice. "You just dump this crazy girl on us? One more mouth to feed, Nick. One more. What're you playing at?"

"Look, Conrad. The information she got from her doll led us to find Rufus the first time, and we followed him here. Then we lost him."

"You lost him? Too busy with your new beau to care for him, I see," Conrad's face was twisted in rage as he spoke.

"Conrad," Ashe started, stepping up beside me with his coat now wrapped tightly around his own body as if to protect him from all this emotion. "It's not Nickie's fault."

"No!" Conrad shouted again, stepping back in line with the others. "Not from you. I don't want to hear from you. You just swoop in here and change everything!"

"We were jumped, Conrad." I spoke calmly, hoping to diffuse the situation. "A couple of vampires jumped us, and we had to fight. That's why we lost them. We have been trying to pick up the trail for hours now, but there has been nothing."

"I know where they are," Cassie said. "My dolly told me to follow the gargoyles."

We all looked down at little Cassie incredulously, and she repeated herself as if we had not heard the first time or had not understood. "We have to follow the gargoyles," she demanded. "You know, the scary monsters on top of the tall buildings."

Conrad looked back at me and shook his head. "Gargoyles, Nick. Really?"

"She didn't lead us wrong before." I defended little Cassie, although it did sound quite mad. "Still, you all should not be out here, there are too many of you for me to protect. Even with Ashe here, if we are attacked again, there's no one to protect you."

"I can hold my own if he can," Conrad said through a snarl, thrusting out his chest and looking at Ashe.

"And what about Franklin and especially Edwin and Cassie?" I asked.

"Well, I've got this," Franklin offered and held up a contraption that looked very much like a crossbow, but it was mounted on his arm and was specifically designed to shoot thin wooden stakes. "I just finished it today. Tested it and everything." He pulled aside his coat to show us several wooden stakes stuck into loops tied into his rope belt.

"I should have known, Franklin." I turned to him. "I had meant to thank you for my boots, by the by. Didn't have much time today, but that's no excuse. They are perfect, and they proved quite effective earlier tonight, they did. You are quite the genius."

"I know," he said without conceit or arrogance. It was as if I said to him, "You are fourteen years old." It was just a fact.

His nose was very red in the cold and every exhaled breath froze in a haze of smoke that quickly dispersed into the surrounding fog. I looked at him with a sense of awe. This young boy was indeed a genius, and I was quite glad to have him on my team.

"As for these two," Conrad continued, creating his own cloud of frozen breath. "We'll watch over them. Keep them between us, a'right? We all want one thing, and that's to find Rufus."

"Very well." I gave in. The wetness from the melted snow on my trousers and legs had refrozen. My legs were stinging as they went numb, and I was starting to shiver again. "Let's move. Cassie, can your dolly direct us?"

"Sure," she said. "My dolly and the gargoyles."

"Of course." I flashed a smile at Conrad. He smiled back. We would be all right. After all, our friendship was stronger than that. Bonded over mutual misery, we would be friends forever. "Edwin, take Cassie's hand and keep her close, all right?"

Edwin did so without hesitation, happy to have a new friend from the looks of it. He was no longer the youngest. Now he had someone to protect as well, and he stepped up to the task admirably.

"That way," Cassie said. "Dolly says to go that way."

And so we went that way, down a rather dark street with few gaslights. The two youngest walked in between us all. Conrad and Franklin flanked them on each side and Ashe and I walked in front and behind them, with Ashe in the back and me leading the way. Two days ago I was a debutante, and now I was a leader of a vampire fighting gang made up of mostly children.

Life was a strange thing.

CHAPTER THIRTEEN

IN WHICH NICKIE NICK
SNEAKS INTO AN INSANE ASYLUM

Cassie stood in the middle of the street looking up to the top of a five-story building. We all surrounded her, waiting to hear what this gargoyle had to say. She had spoken to half a dozen over the last hour, and I had no doubt everyone else felt as foolish as I did. Even though I believed this strange little girl had some second sight or supernatural insight, it still felt quite strange to be standing in the middle of an abandoned London street in the wee hours of Christmas morning talking to a gargoyle.

"But it's getting very cold," Cassie shouted up to the stone statue, who was indeed as still as stone, but each of her replies were as if she was conversing with it. "Don't you know any more?" she continued, "I'm really tired and really cold, and I want to go to bed. Please help us." Her broken doll hung from its remaining arm at Cassie's side. Edwin still held her other hand.

"I'm tired, too," Edwin said.

"Quiet down there. We're tryin' to sleep," someone yelled from one of the second story windows.

"We need to go," I whispered to Cassie. "Which way."

"That way." She pointed up and around the next corner. We were now nearly back in Lambeth, near Kennington Road, which is where Cassie said to turn. My own house was but a few blocks away, and I truly longed for the comfort and warmth of my bed. I wanted to be just another seventeen-year-old debutante waking up to Christmas morning in a few hours. Sitting by the fire with my parents and having a hot breakfast. Perhaps an apple tart or two as well. Opening gifts. Even an afternoon with Lord Godwyn was starting to appeal to me, despite the company he kept. At least I would be warm.

One look at Ashe cured me of that thought, however. Forever patient. He had not complained once and kept a constant look out for danger. His eyes scanned the streets and alleyways for any sense of movement, and we had all been lucky that there had been none.

Several other gargoyles and even a weather vane guided us down Kennington Road, which still had a few carriages out and about even at this late hour, until we came upon what looked like a large park on the left. Through the trees, a dome glowed in the hazy winter night. It was like the dome on St. Paul's, but much smaller. The rest of the building was buried in the fog.

"This way," Cassie said after checking with a gaslamp post. She led us right up to the wrought iron, waist-high fence. "In there," she continued. "They went in there."

"Perfect. Thank you, Cassie. You did really well," I said to her, stooping down to give her a hug.

"Can I go to sleep now?" She started to sag in my arms, laying her head on my shoulder.

I looked up at Conrad. "Will you get them home and into bed?" I asked him, but he was not having any of it.

"You're not going in there alone with him." He sneered at Ashe, then looked back at me. "Do you know what this place is?" Conrad asked. "This is Bethlehem Asylum, Nick. My mother is a patient here. It's a madhouse." He looked at me in my Protector gear then at Cassie, who was holding her broken china doll closely to her chest and sucking her thumb, then at Franklin who had his crossbow arm out at the ready. "Although, perhaps this is the very place for all of us."

"Conrad, we have no idea what we will find in there. You will be safer at home."

"Nickie," Ashe said. "I think Conrad is right. They should stay with us."

"What?" I felt a little betrayed. "Care to explain?"

"It is at least an hour's walk from here to the flat, and the streets at this hour are not a safe place to be."

"They found us well enough on their own," I said, although I knew that had been pure luck on their part, and I was not willing to risk them being so lucky on the way back, especially now that we were twice as far from the flat as before.

"We can hold our own." Conrad furrowed his brow again. "Stop treating me like a child, Nickie. I'm a man. Only a year behind you."

"Fine, but you boys are staying in the park, safely tucked away. Ashe and I will go inside and find Rufus."

"Let's see what we are dealing with first," Franklin offered. "I doubt you will be able to just walk in. You may need us yet."

"Yes, we should all go," Conrad said and jumped over the wrought iron fence before I could argue further. He reached over and lifted up little Cassie. Ashe lifted Edwin over, then went over himself. Franklin and I followed suit.

Random pieces of green grass poked out from the snow, which looked golden in the glow of the gaslamps. As we moved further from the street, however, the light dimmed. Before long, we were walking in complete darkness, towards the light of the dome. Silence, except for our feet crunching in the snow, surrounded us.

"Wait," Ashe whispered and put both hands out, stopping everyone behind him. We all stopped and held our breaths. "There is someone there," Ashe said.

Edwin hugged Cassie tight, and she hid her face in his coat.

There, in the courtyard of the great red brick building before us, a solitary lantern swung back and forth in the foggy darkness. The night watchman on his rounds. I followed the swinging light as it went down the length of the building. Once he was far enough away from us, Ashe stepped back and whispered in my ear, "See that tree there, the big one." He pointed up ahead a few yards, and I nodded. "Get the children there, in the shadow of the tree. Conrad and I will keep watch for the lantern."

"Follow me," I said to Edwin and Franklin. Once at the tree, I saw that there was a fairly large, low hanging branch. I lifted Cassie up onto it, then Edwin. At least they would not be snatched straight away if they were up off the ground. Franklin stood leaning against the trunk, crossbow at the ready. "Stay in the shadow of the tree, all right? If the man with the lantern comes anywhere near you, just stay very, very still. He will not be able to see you if you stay still and quiet. All right?"

They both nodded. Edwin put his arm protectively around Cassie. "It's all right if you want to sleep a little, Cassie. I'll stay awake and make sure you are safe."

My heart swelled beneath my corset. These children should not be in this dangerous situation. I shouldn't be here either, for that matter, but here we were. "Ready?" I asked Ashe.

He nodded.

"Conrad, would you stay here on the other side of the path, just to help keep them safe?" I hoped that giving Conrad the responsibility of keeping the younger ones safe would help keep him out of harm's way as well.

No luck.

"My mum's in there, Nickie. If we're bustin' in anyway, why can't we bust her out as well? She shouldn't be in there. I've heard stories. Horrible stories, Nick. She's not mad. You know that. Right, Nickie?"

"Quiet," Ashe repeated, and we all melted into the shadows. There was no way the night watchman could have gone around that huge building already. It was at least an entire block long and goodness knows how deep, but sure enough, another lantern light came swinging into view.

"There must be more than one," Ashe whispered to us. "Maybe three or four."

"Then we will have to be quick," I said. "As soon as he is down to the end, we go."

Ashe nodded again.

"You stay here," I added to Conrad.

He scowled, but didn't argue.

The lantern came closer, and we all held our breaths until he passed.

Conrad just stood there staring at me, and I could see the resentment on his face. But I couldn't look out for him and search for Rufus and watch my own back. It was best that he stayed behind.

I nodded to Ashe, a signal to move. We each moved quickly, faster than a human, which is why we didn't notice that Conrad had not stayed behind as told. We reached the door and Conrad was still in the middle of the courtyard heading towards us. It was too risky to shout out to him, so I just let him come and prayed the others would be safe in their hiding places.

The door was locked, but Ashe was able to open it with one of his many skeleton keys. We ducked inside just as the lantern light appeared at the far end of the building again.

"What do you think you are doing?" I whispered to Conrad after the door was closed behind us. "You could have gotten us all caught, then where would Rufus and your mother be? Still here, stuck in here."

"I'm not leaving her in here, Nick," Conrad breathed.

Obviously unable to persuade him with reason, I turned back to the task.

"This place is enormous." I looked up into the great dome above us. The foyer opened all the way up to the dome which started four stories above us and stretched up at least as much again. The most awful stench suddenly hit me. "Ugh! What is that smell?"It was quite similar to the smell in the sewers and down by the river.

I tiptoed to the corner of the hallway and looked down each side. What had looked like a rather nice building from the outside, not all that different from my own home (albeit ten times the size) was a foul dungeon on the inside. The hallways were lined with iron bars. Several cages of various sizes were in the hallway as well. Everything was so very dark that I could barely make out the edges, but something white was moving around inside.

"Oh, my god," I gasped, covering my mouth and shrinking back into Ashe. "People! Those cages on the grounds have people inside them. It's like a prison or some horrible torture chamber in here. Oh! And that stench."

"They have people living in their own filth," Ashe offered.

A single tear spilled over onto Conrad's cheek. "Can you see why I couldn't leave my mother in here, Nick? Do you understand now?"

"I do, Conrad. Of course I understand," I whispered back, "but we have to find her first."

"What are we waiting for then?" He angrily wiped the tear away and marched past me down the right hallway.

"Go with him, will you?" I asked Ashe. "I'm going up there." I pointed up into the dome. On the back side of the building, after the four stories of prison just at the base of the dome was a door. "Be careful," I added and kissed him on the cheek. He just nodded and followed Conrad without a word.

Before I could make it to the staircase across the hall, a loud voice shouted, "No! They've come to get me! They've come to take me! Please don't let them take me!"

After that, an uproar followed unlike I had ever heard. All the inmates from the first story chimed in, each yelling something different. Some clanged on the bars of the cells others just screamed. Blood-curdling screams, like the sound of pure, abject horror.

It was apparently contagious, as the next three stories above me followed suit.

The entire place suddenly lit up, and I caught sight of a nurse down at the far left end turning a gas key in the wall. She held a metal rod, and I saw her shock one of the inmates with it.

I shrunk against the foyer wall, but I no longer had the darkness to hide me. I could see Ashe and Conrad still looking from cell to cell, more quickly now. There was no doubt the nurse had seen them.

So I waited and I breathed.

A moment later, the nurse came rushing past me, shocking-rod in hand. Without thinking or even having any semblance of a plan, I jumped out, grabbed her around the mouth to keep her from screaming, although she would not have been heard over this mayhem anyway, took the rod from her with the other, and pulled her back against the wall with me.

Now what?

Think, Nickie. Think!

I didn't know what to do with her. I knew how to deal with vampires, and I think I would even do all right with a demon, but what would I do with this human?

All around us the cacophony of cries and screams continued, and I struggled to hold on to the remaining shred of hope that we would all somehow get out alive.

CHAPTER FOURTEEN

IN WHICH NICKIE NICK DISCOVERS A MAD-PSYCHIATRIST AT WORK

The only thing I could do to buy us more time was to take the nurse down with me to Ashe and Conrad. Perhaps they would have an idea. I had thought about shoving her outside and locking the door, but that would just alert the two or three night watchmen. Although, I was quite sure they had been already alerted to something amiss with all this noise.

The woman squirmed in my arms and made it quite difficult to walk, but I made it down the hall to Ashe and Conrad.

"What do we do now?" I yelled over the patients. The ones who had wiggled out of their straightjackets were grabbing at us, dirty, white, pointed arms flapped wildly. The others were trying to get out of their own straightjackets. Their elbows flailed, pulling against the restraints that kept their arms wrapped around their bodies.

"Down here," Ashe yelled. "An empty cell. Get her in here."

The nurse struggled more fiercely than ever, and I had to drop her shocking-rod to contain her and force her into the filthy cell.

"Let's see how she likes it." Conrad's cheeks were stained with tears and there was angry fire in his eyes. He snatched the rod away from one of the patients in an elongated cage on the floor who had picked it up and had been shocking himself with it. The cage was barely big enough for the patient, so he had to hold the rod outside the cage with his arms through the bars.

"Conrad, no!" The sound of my voice was drowned out by the renewed cheering, shouting, and screaming when the surrounding patients saw what Conrad intended to do. The nurse realized what was coming too late, for she was pressed up against the bars begging to be let out. That's until Conrad shocked her, vibrating her struggling figure against the bars as the electricity surged through her. The nurse's painful screams were lost in the din of the other patients. Her hands grasped the bars more tightly than before and saliva dribbled out of her mouth.

Conrad shocked her a second time and shouted, "Is this how you treat my mother? Is this what you do to her here?" Tears streamed down his face.

I pulled the shocking-rod away from Conrad and the nurse fell away from the bars, collapsing on the floor.

"No," he shouted. "She deserves this!"

But before I could respond, I saw the night nurses from the upper stories pointing down towards us, and that feeling of dread crept back into my chest.

"We have got to get moving," I shouted to them both and grabbed Conrad by the hand, dragging him behind me. Ashe was not far behind.

As I reached the stairway, the three other night nurses, two of them male, descended upon us, their own rods at the ready. I thrust the rod I had towards the first nurse, and it hit him but there was no shock. Conrad must have drained it.

He lunged at me, thrusting his weapon, and the image of the vibrating nurse came to mind. It looked like it really hurt. After dodging his attempt and tossing the dead rod aside, I disarmed the first nurse with a roundhouse kick, knocking the rod from his hands. I kicked it across the aisle and noticed out of the corner of my eye that another patient picked it up. The nurse came at me again, and I stopped him with a punch that sent him flying into the adjacent cell's bars. The patient therein grabbed ahold of him and commenced biting off his ear. The fresh screams of the nurse were quickly lost in the cacophony of sound. After a moment, he collapsed unconscious from shock. That horrible coppery blood smell mixed with the burning flesh, urine, feces, and all the rest. I held my breath, trying not to wretch.

I turned, ready for the next, but saw that Ashe had taken out the second male nurse, who now lay unconscious on the floor. The third, the second woman, was held in a choke hold by Conrad. He was screaming, "Where is Laura Hannon? Where is Laura Hannon? Take me to her. Now!" He was holding the shocking-rod inches from her waist, and I think she got the message.

She nodded and shouted over the noise, "Third floor. She's on three. I'll take you to her, just please don't hurt me!"

Conrad walked up the stairs with the nurse in his grasp. Ashe and I followed. I chanced a look back, and the other two nurses were still unconscious. They likely would be for quite some time. I took a moment to cover my nose with the sleeve of my coat and take in a deep breath. While all the other horrid smells were there, it was masked momentarily by the scent of leather from my coat.

When we reached the third floor I told Conrad, "Get your mum, we're going up to the dome. I think it's where Rufus is being kept."

"How do you know?"

"Call it a strong feeling," I said, unable to explain the mysterious force urging me to go up into the dome room.

"Meet you back on the first floor by the door. Don't hurt her," I ordered, indicting the nurse. "And don't jeopardize the safety of the others outside anymore than we already have."

Conrad nodded and stayed on the third floor while Ashe and I continued up the stairs. When we reached the fourth floor, there was a metal staircase leading up to that lone door. Just as we stepped onto the first step, the door opened and out came a man in a white lab coat.

Ashe stopped and pulled me close to him.

Over this man's left shoulder, a leather pauldron was strapped in place. It had copper pipes running from a pressure gauge on the top of the shoulder down to another contraption on his arm. He wore goggles, similar to the ones I had on, only his had several magnifying lenses on protruding arms. He pushed the goggles up onto his forehead and stretched out his arms.

In an instant, the entire place went silent.

Ashe let go of me and stood at attention next to me.

"Come," the man said looking at us, and Ashe did.

I followed.

The man didn't give us a second look, but turned and went back into the room. I stepped into the room just after Ashe did, and looked around.

It was large, much like a warehouse, but it was most definitely not a warehouse. It was a laboratory. Lined up on both sides were the blocks of men, and there was Rufus in the very front with some other children. They all had the same blank stare as before, and so did Ashe.

Not good.

This man had some sort of hold on them all, like he was controlling their thoughts and their actions. I was unaffected, at least for the time being, I had better act as if I was with them until I knew more.

"You there." The man pointed to one of the larger men in the group, "Go restore order blow. Tend to the hurt orderlies and release Gladys from the end cell on level one."

How did he know about that? I wondered.

The man nodded, turned, and walked out without a word.

"Sit," the man in control said, and the entire room all sat down at once, including Ashe.

I was a split second behind everyone else, but the man's back had been turned, so he didn't notice.

He approached a long table full of instruments, vials, test tubes, and the like. In fact, upon a closer look, racks and racks of test tubes filled the long, steel table. At one end a large beaker filled with a black bubbling liquid hung in a wire rack, suspended over a flame. At the other end, where this bizarre man situated himself by arranging some papers and picking up an ink pen, a phonograph dominated the corner. But it was not really a phonograph, certainly not the kind father had in his library that played musical cylinders of Beethoven. This one had a much smaller horn, and instead of music coming out of it, this man spoke into it. He wound up the crank on the side, which caused some belt-driven gears to spin, which, in turn, rotated the cylinder. An arm drug across the cylinder as he spoke, making a deep scratching sound.

"Dr. Zachariah Pilkington, supplemental," he said. "A great disturbance below interrupted me earlier, and I have yet to discover the cause of it, other than finding two strangers at my doorstep. I mesmerized them along with the others, and will soon be learning what this is all about. Until then, allow me to complete my thought from before. The results of the past few days have further confirmed what I learned on the Grand Tour. The human mind, of course, can indeed be controlled utterly, as theorized and proven by my mentor Dr. Braid. Not only can it be controlled, but that hypnotic control can be extended en masse when mixed with sorcery. My mesmerized, zombie army has reached near fifty sane persons in just a few days. They, and the entire asylum, are at my command. I shall be ready to execute my plan by New Year's Day."

I didn't wait to hear what this plan was, as this Dr. Pilkington was obviously as insane as any of his patients, only infinitely more powerful. I moved up behind quickly and tapped him on the shoulder.

He turned, shocked to see that I was not mesmerized.

"I shall be taking my friends out of here now." I punched him square across the jaw. His head hit the side of the table with a disturbing crack, and he fell to the floor unconscious. All his "zombies," as he called them, remained still. Unaffected.

I grabbed Rufus and Ashe by the hands and headed for the door, but just as I reached it, the zombie who had gone to check on the damage returned with Conrad and a woman I didn't recognize. I could only assume it was his mother. The zombie stepped right past me and fell back in line with the others.

Conrad and his mother just stood there, staring blankly at nothing.

Great.

I somehow managed to get them all outside, pushing two with one hand and leading two with the other, only to be caught by one of the circling guards. He shouted out an alarm to the others and then picked up a whistle dangling from the breast of his uniform. Blowing it wildly, he came at me, billy club raised.

The four with me didn't move.

As the guard swung his club at me, I ducked and spun around, knocking his feet out from under him. He hit the ground hard. Perhaps a little too hard, for he was not moving at all.

Two other guards came running towards us from either end of the building. I pushed my four zombified friends forward as quickly as their ambling gait would allow, trying to get them across the courtyard before the other guards could run the length of the long building.

I didn't make it.

With a forceful push, I propelled Ashe and the others forward a few more feet and prepared to face the oncoming guards.

Both were loudly blowing their whistles in the most annoying way, although I didn't understand who else they hoped to alert. Clubs raised, they rushed me from opposite directions. As I prepared to fight them both, a better plan came to mind. When they reached me, I merely stepped back at the last moment. They ran into each other, which distracted them for but a moment. But it was enough.

Franklin came out from behind the stone gate, crossbow in hand. Edwin was right behind him with Cassie protectively by his side. Franklin shot one of the guards in the leg as he scrambled up and charged. The other, I faced. He swung his billy club and I ducked, throwing a punch into his stomach. He doubled over and I jabbed him with an upper cut. He went down just as hard as the first, his jaw split in two, broken. That last punch was too hard. I had hit him with my full force, now he would likely never speak again, if he even survived.

This was not my night.

Yet, the guards were taken care of. Two unconscious. One writhing in pain.

I turned back to my responsibility and pushed my four zombie friends through the gates.

"You found Rufus!" Franklin said.

"I found quite a lot inside that place."

"Who is this?" Franklin asked, regarding the woman.

"Conrad's mother, I think."

"Conrad?" Franklin said, but Conrad just stared straight ahead along with Ashe, his mother, and Rufus.

"They are under some sort of spell." I tried to collect my thoughts and put everything into words. Finally, I admitted, "I cannot explain fully now. Listen, can you get them back to yours? I will meet you there shortly with some help. I hope."

"How? I mean. Just me, Edwin, and Cassie with them?"

"They seem to go where you direct them, albeit slowly. Edwin and Cassie, each of you take two by the hand and lead them home. Franklin, you walk behind them with your crossbow ready, but hidden."

He nodded.

"Be smart. Stay safe. I will see what I can do about breaking this spell and meet you at the flat before dawn."

Edwin and Cassie each took two by the hand, Edwin with Conrad and Rufus, and Cassie between Ashe and Conrad's mum. Franklin walked behind them.

I watched them disappear into the darkness before turning toward my house, only a few blocks away. If there was a spell that needed breaking, we needed a witch.

Chapter Fifteen

In Which Nickie Nick
Learns More About Witchcraft

"They are under a spell you say?" Fanny said groggily. I had sneaked back in through the pantry and woken her up. It was early Christmas morning, and dawn was quickly approaching.

"He said something about mesmerism and sorcery."

"Mesmerism and sorcery? Oh my," she yawned. "I remember hearing about that man Mesmer from when I was a girl. Well, I mean he's long dead now, isn't he? But one of his best students was a Scotsman. Braid, I think."

"Yes! He mentioned a Dr. Braid. Said it was his mentor."

"Braid was ridiculed for toying with the supernatural, which gained the attention of the coven. He worked hard to refute that rumor, though. Insisting that it was only science. But this man, you say, he is using sorcery?"

"That's what he said, Fanny. We've got to go." The boys needed us, and here she was just laying in bed talking about the past.

"Go? For heaven's sake. Go where? It's nearly dawn!" Fanny turned over and pulled the covers over her head.

"My friends are in trouble, and I think you can help with your powers. Please, Fanny, help break the spell. I don't know who else to turn to."

"Certainly the effects will wear off after a bit. We must get you dressed for Christmas morning. There are gifts!"

Even my best sad-eyes look was not budging the woman. She didn't yet understand the magnitude of the situation.

"Fanny! Have you been listening to me? My friends are hypnotized! Turned into some kind of mesmerized zombies, and there are more. Nearly fifty more that I saw! And if Dr. Pilkington is to be allowed to continue, he shall mesmerize more. He's building an army for something. I don't know for what, but it cannot be good, Fanny. Please!" I pleaded, shaking her now.

"Very well. Very well." She threw her quilt off and swung her legs over the bed. "Collect my skirts, will you?" She pointed over to her dresser on top of which lay her black skirt and blouse. She twisted her long, fuzzy red hair into a tight bun and taking a hair stick from off her nightstand, fixed her hair in place. I placed her skirt and blouse on the bed next to her.

"Pull up the floorboards," she instructed. "There's a package down there, bound in black satin. Bring it to me." She continued getting dressed, as I did as she asked. I pulled up the floorboards beneath her rug, where she had shown me a few days ago. It already seemed like weeks, but it really had only been a few days. Strange how such significant events can make one feel that the person they were just a few days ago seemed like another lifetime.

"It is not here." I saw only her bundle of weapons. Even when I picked them up and looked underneath, I saw nothing else.

"To the side." She buttoned up her blouse, then pointed. "The right side."

Reaching my arm into the opening and then under the floor, I found it. There, just as she said, was a package, bound in black satin and tied off with a black satin ribbon. Much larger than I had thought, for I didn't know the cubby hidden beneath the floorboards was so large. The opening to the secret compartment was just the width and length of one plank, but the cubby beneath was quite extensive. There was much more hidden beneath there, I gathered.

The package was about the size of two bread loaves, and I couldn't imagine what was inside. It felt rather too light to be weapons.

She took the black satin package from me and tucked it under her arm. "Ready?" she asked.

"Whenever you are," I answered, replacing the floorboard.

"How far is this place?"

"A few miles. Oh, no." I remembered that she couldn't move as fast as I could. It would take us well over an hour to get there on foot.

"Indeed. A few miles," she said disapprovingly. "You expect me to walk a few miles in the freezing cold of Christmas morning? In these boots?" She pointed to her pointed toe boots. "Nonsense," she continued. "I shall wake Lucian. He will drive us."

"But my parents," I started to protest, but she put her hand up to stop me.

"Lucian can be quite discreet," she assured me.

We rode in the carriage and the clacking sound of the wheels on the cobblestones broke the silent magic of Christmas morning. Soon families all over London would be waking to open the gifts Father Christmas had brought them last night. Such a simple life they led, unaware of the dangers around them. Just as mine had been a few days ago.

Oh! To be home asleep in my warm bed, dreaming about reindeer and mince pies and crackers full of bon bons. I would have left out cookies and carrots for Father Christmas and his reindeer. Instead, here I was, falling for a vampire and trying to thwart the plans of a mad psychiatrist from turning London into a zombie army.

Yes. Things certainly had changed.

"Just over there." I leaned out the window, shouting up to Lucian. He nodded and pulled over. "Quickly," I said to Fanny. She tucked her package under her arm again and climbed out of the carriage.

"Not a word to the master or mistress, Lucian. All right?" Fanny said, waving her hand in the air. Lucian looked lost for a moment, much like the zombies did, and then he snapped back to lucidity.

"Yah!" he shouted to the horses and snapped the reigns. Lucian drove them away without another look to us.

"What did you do to him?" I asked Fanny.

"Well, he cannot tell what he does not know, can he?" she smiled slightly. It was a mischievous smile, and I wondered how many times she had used that little trick on me or my family. Perhaps she could teach me, as that would be quite handy with mother.

"This way," I whispered, pointing to the doorway. We entered and went up the stairs, knocking on the door to the right when we reached the second level. Franklin answered.

"Hello Nickie. We only just got in ourselves. How did you get here so fast?" He looked at Fanny with uncertainty. They had come to mistrust adults, and for good reason. Most adults wanted to use them for cheap labor or to exploit them in other horrible ways.

"Carriage," I answered, then followed with some brief introductions. "Fanny, this is Franklin and Cassie."

"So this is Fanny the Nanny." Franklin said. "So nice to finally meet you, ma'am."

Fanny gave me a look. She really did hate that moniker.

"Just Fanny will do, and the pleasure is mine, dear boy. Nichole speaks very highly of you and your creations."

Franklin beamed.

Cassie stood in the corner, holding her dolly tightly. "He's coming," she warned.

"What did you say, child?" Fanny asked her, moving closer to Cassie.

Cassie seemed to want to disappear into the wall, for she shrank back and pulled her dolly closer, hiding half her face with the doll's broken one.

"My dolly says the bad man is awake again, and he is looking for us."

Fanny looked back at me with a curious look.

"Her doll speaks to her," I explained matter-of-factly. "So do statues and gargoyles and even weather vanes. It is a thing."

"I see," Fanny said politely. Fanny always treated people as equals, whether they were above her station or below. I loved that about her. She didn't treat children as lesser people, but rather regarded them with respect.

We walked fully into the living area and the four zombified friends were each sitting in a different chair, staring.

"This is Ashe, Rufus, you know Conrad, and this, we think, is Conrad's mother." I pointed to each as I said their names. "He went into the asylum to rescue her. I cannot blame him now. Fanny, it was an awful place. I didn't know such horror existed." But then so much horror had been brought to my attention since I turned seventeen. Horror and wonder, both. Seeing them all like that was quite disturbing, but fascinating that someone could do that. Horrible that someone would.

"Indeed. I have heard stories of those places, my lamb. Of course, we witches are no stranger to ill treatment, but what I hear about these asylums. It is a special kind of hell."

"She's a witch?" Franklin said, not at all scared, but rather intrigued.

"Indeed I am, young lad, and I hear you are quite the inventor." Fanny folded her hands over her skirts and turned to Franklin.

"That's true." He took a moment before continuing, sizing her up. "I have never met a witch before."

"And I have never met an inventor before. I trust we shall both learn a great deal from each other." She became very quiet for a moment, but recovered herself quickly enough and said, "I need a place to work. Is there a kitchen?"

"Through here," Franklin said. "It is my workshop as well. Can you help my friends?"

"I will certainly try."

Franklin led Fanny into the kitchen and I followed.

He had really taken over the kitchen in the short time they had been there. It looked similar to the mad psychiatrist's laboratory, only instead of bubbling potions, test tube racks, copious notes, and the like, the kitchen was filled with junk, or what looked like junk to the untrained eye. To Franklin, these were all just raw materials. Every surface was covered with metal pieces, scrap clothing and leather, coins, and more junk than I could begin to describe. Sketches scrawled on scraps of paper were nailed all over the walls. There was a small table in the center of the room, on which more scribbled sketches and junk sat, but Franklin cleared off a space with a sweeping motion, pushing all his work to one side.

Fanny, who looked rather overwhelmed by all the junk, sat down and placed her black satin wrapped package on the cleared space. She was far too polite to say anything about the mess, but the shock in her eyes betrayed her feelings to me, at least.

"Thank you, Franklin. You have got quite the work-shop here." She started to unwrap the large package.

"I know. It's really great, isn't it? I can finally get something done, thanks to Ashe. He got us this place."

"Did he?" Fanny asked, looking up at me.

No one knew Ashe was a vampire but me, and I was not sure if they should know. Ever. As I was still unsure how I felt about it.

"Yep," Franklin said. "I was already able to make something else for you, Nickie," he continued, turning to me.

"Really? When? We have been out all night."

"Well, before we went out, obviously. I haven't tested them yet, so they might need a little tweaking." Franklin took a strange contraption off the counter. There were straps, as if they wrapped around one's arm or maybe leg, and there was a wooden stake set in a metal part. Franklin took off his coat and strapped the thing on his arm. The stake ran along the inside of his forearm, and a metal ring connected to a wire dangled from it.

Franklin threaded this ring over his middle finger, and with a quick flex of his hand, the stake shot out. He jabbed forward, as if staking a vampire, then relaxed his hand. The stake went back to its original place along his forearm.

"That's brilliant, Franklin! Truly brilliant!"

"Oh my, Nicole. You certainly were not exaggerating about this one. He is quite the genius. Indeed," Fanny said.

"Thanks." Franklin took compliments well. "I think I want to tweak it more before you take it out. I wouldn't want you to accidentally puncture your hand with it."

"That would not be good, no." I smiled down at him. I resisted the urge to tussle his hair, for he truly looked like a little boy, even at fourteen. But I do believe he was more mature than anyone else in this house. Save, perhaps, Fanny.

She had unwrapped her package fully now. Laying on the table, the pool of unwrapped satin nestled several bundles herbs, some tinctures, a few candles, a box of matches, two knifes, and a wand. She took the two knives out and placed them aside. I went to reach for one out of curiosity, it had a pewter pentagram affixed to its wooden hilt. Before I could touch it, Fanny slapped my hand away.

"Don't touch," she scolded. "That athame has been handed down to me through ten generations of witches.

No one but its witch shall touch it, or it would lose its power."

"All right!" I rubbed my hand, "but, ow!"

"Now, generally to break a spell, one needs arrowroot and chamomile." She ignored me. "Franklin, is there something in which I can mix this? And perhaps a piece of wood or something on which I can cut these herbs as well."

Franklin put down his spring-loaded stake contraption and fetched Fanny a small, cracked ceramic bowl and a piece of scrap wood from his piles of junk. He went right to each one respectively, as if he had his own system of organization in this chaos.

"Thank you, Franklin." She picked up the bound herbs and pulled out a dried bundle. It had dark, green leaves and a bulbous root. Breaking off one of those bulbs, she commenced to cut it in to small pieces using her special knife and then put the pieces into the cracked ceramic bowl. Picking up one of the tincture bottles, she added a few drops of a yellowish, thick liquid to the pieces of root in the bowl. She stirred the two with the knife and whispered words over it as she did so. Then, picking up the wooden wand, she waved it over the mixture and whispered more words.

If I had not seen what I had seen over the past few days, I would have thought this was all quite mad. But this was not mad at all, for I had a new definition of madness. This might just save my friends.

A puff of grey smoke burst out of the concoction, making me and Franklin jump back a foot. Then Fanny put the wand down. "That should do it."

She handed me the bowl, and I looked down into the mixture, which looked very different than the ingredients she had so recently put in. It was a dark purple mush, still slightly smoking. After wiping it off on her skirts, Fanny wrapped up her precious knife back in the black satin, along with the other herbs and supplies.

"What are you waiting for, child? There is not time to waste!" she scolded, shooing me into the next room.

Cassie was cowering in the corner repeating, "The bad man is coming. The bad man is coming. The bad man is coming."

The other four were just as we had left them. Catatonic.

"Take a little on the tip of your finger, Nicole, and touch it to each of their tongues."

Ew. I thought, but I knew there was no time for squeamishness now. I did as Fanny asked, starting with Conrad's mum, just in case something went wrong. It was awful of me to both doubt Fanny's expertise and judge Conrad's mum as the most expendable, but this all was certainly new territory for me.

I dipped my forefinger in the purple mush, and it was warm. Handing the bowl to Franklin, who was standing beside me to see what would happen, I pried Conrad's mum's mouth open with my newly freed hand. Touching the concoction to her tongue, she awoke almost immediately.

"Who are you!" she exclaimed. "Where am I?" She was frantic and frightened.

I had not thought about the ramifications of waking the insane one first.

"Shhhh," I tried. "I'm a friend of your son's. See?" I pointed to Conrad. "There is your son. He rescued you out of that horrible place, remember?"

"Conrad? Oh my boy! Conrad!" Conrad, of course, didn't move, which only caused her to freak out even more. "What have you done to him? What have you done!" She got up and came at me, and I had to forcibly shove her back into the chair and hold her down as she continued to struggle.

"Just wait, lady." I pinned her wrists down on the chair's arms. "I didn't do this to Conrad, but I'm going to help him if you stop squiggling for a moment. All right?"

She quieted down and nodded.

I dipped my finger back into the mush, which was considerably cooler now, and then repeated the ritual on Conrad. He awoke as well, but much slower than his mother. It must already be losing some potency. I had better awaken the others quickly.

"Nickie, what the–" Conrad started, but then his mother knocked me out of the way and gathered him up in her arms.

"You came for me! Oh, my boy, you came for me. Thank you! Thank you! I'm better now. Please don't make me go back to that place. Please!"

"No, Mum. You don't have to go back. You will live here with us," Conrad said, and they were both crying. I felt my own tears coming at this heartfelt reunion, but I cleared my throat and awakened Rufus, who took even longer to wake up. Franklin shoved the bowl back in my hand after Rufus was lucid again, gathering him up in an embrace as well.

Now came Ashe. I didn't know how the concoction would work on the undead, and I didn't know if I should tell Fanny about the anomaly or not. Dipping my finger in the now cold mush, I tried it on him just as I had the others. After setting the bowl down and trying to block out Cassie's cries of "The bad man is coming" and the others' joyous chattering, I forced open his cold lips and put my finger against his tongue.

Nothing.

Dreadful thoughts filled my mind again, just like before when I thought he was dead. I couldn't lose him.

I loved him. I knew that now and I didn't care if he was a vampire or a human. I loved him.

Everyone had quieted down (except Cassie) and was now watching to see if Ashe would wake up.

The tears started to burn behind my eyes. I cleaned out the bottom of the bowl where the mush was already hardening, and then tried again, smearing the purple paste over the front of his tongue.

Please wake up, Ashe. Please, I thought frantically, but there was no movement until...

His lips clamped down over my finger and his eyes caught mine. He ran his tongue down the underside of my finger, sucking gently, as he pulled back from it. He smiled and I blushed.

"Well hello there Nickie Nick," he said. "What a lovely sight you are."

"Ahem," Fanny cleared her throat, and I turned to see her with her arms crossed glaring down at me.

"Um," I stammered. "Fanny, this is Ashe."

"How do you do?" He stood, took her hand, and kissed it.

Fanny went from being flattered and even blushing slightly one moment to enraged the next. "He is a vampire," she shouted, snatching her hand away.

All the chatter in the room stopped. Even Cassie stopped chanting "The bad man is coming" for a moment. They all looked at Ashe, who looked at me.

Although everyone was waiting for me to stake him, as I was The Protector, after all, I stepped in front of him protectively. "It's all right. Everyone, just calm down," I added as the chatter started back up. "He is a vampire. I know, but he is a good vampire. I think."

"You think? You stupid girl. Has this beast brainwashed you?" Fanny scolded. "He just looks at you with those soulful eyes and you get weak in the knees? Foolish girl. You are The Protector! It is your sacred duty to slay vampires and other creatures of darkness!"

"I know!" I shouted back at Fanny, hoping it would keep her quiet.

Conrad looked at me as if I had personally betrayed him. No doubt my attention to Ashe hurt even more now that Conrad knew what he really was, that I would choose a "monster" over him.

The others still stared at me with open mouths, unsure what to think.

"It is not his fault. All right?" I defended him against the group. It seemed like the right thing to do. Always for the underdog, as Fanny liked to say. "He was attacked and turned just six months ago, and he fights them, too. Right?" I said, turning to Ashe for back up.

"What she speaks is true. I hunt the creatures, and I'm not proud of what I am."

The look on his face was a mixture of embarrassment and sadness. Had we been alone, I would have reached out to him and comforted him, kissing his sadness away. But we were not alone.

"It is true. We killed vampires together earlier tonight. We need Ashe with us for this fight. He is the strongest fighter we have, next to me, and we need him to defeat this crazy Dr. Pilkington chap. One vampire is not a problem against this madman. Can we all just keep from judging Ashe until this is all over?"

No one looked convinced, but Ashe's trial was postponed for the moment when Cassie screamed, "He's here! He's here!"

The front door splintered with a loud crash. Dr. Pilkington stepped into the room with two orderlies and said, "That will be sooner than you think."

CHAPTER SIXTEEN

IN WHICH NICKIE NICK MUST SAVE CHRISTMAS

"How did you find us?" I asked, trying to stall before he put everyone in a trance. Only I would be immune because of Conrad's charmed compass, and I couldn't make Fanny's antidote to wake everyone. I stepped forward and nudged Fanny as I passed her by, hoping she would do something to protect us all the way she protected me via the pocket compass and amulet. She got the hint, for I heard her start whispering. I placed myself between her and the crazy doctor, so he couldn't see her mumbling her incantations.

"Do tell, doctor. How did you find us?" I repeated, mostly to cover up Fanny's spell casting. I just had to stall for a few minutes.

"I could see through all their eyes, as I'm completely connected with those I control and can see what they see. That's, until you broke the spell. Do tell how you managed to do that." Dr. Pilkington slowly inched off his gloves by plucking at each finger separately, then pulling the entire thing off. He repeated the action with the other hand, and even I felt drawn into his slow, methodical movement. He was trying to get all our focus at once.

"It is not going to work." I nodded to his gloves.

"What is not going to work, my dear?" he said, looking at me. The two orderlies, each holding a shocking rod, helped the doctor off with his coat, which had just been draped over his shoulders. Still sitting on his right shoulder was the brass contraption I had seen before. Once his gloves and coat were both off, I saw that there was another attachment running from the contraption to his hand. Like Franklin's spring-loaded stake, it was some sort of release cord looped around his middle finger.

"You will not be able to hypnotize us with that thing. Not this time."

"Seems it didn't work on you in the first place, my dear. I shall have to be more careful in the future to ensure no one is protected by magic." His eyes flicked over my shoulder to Fanny, who was still whispering. "I see you have a witch among you. Touché."

"Yes, we do. A very old and powerful witch." Fanny nudged me from behind after I said "old." "We have more power among us than you think," I continued, posturing.

"So I gathered, otherwise, how could you have possibly escaped my mind?"

"Your mind seems like a very scary place to be."

His eyes narrowed.

Probably best not to make him too angry until Fanny could finish.

"Scary, but brilliant," Franklin said. "I'm an inventor, too. And I bet I could learn a lot from you, if you're interested in an apprentice."

"Franklin?" I really hoped that this was just some false flattery delay tactic.

"Brilliant, you say? You think so?" His eyes had widened again and there was joy there.

"Indeed, doctor. Your intellect is quite impressive. I made this here, see?" Franklin held up the crossbow arm apparatus. "A far cry from yours, of course. Tell me about yours. Please."

If I was not mistaken, I would swear the doctor blushed a little.

"It is nothing, really. Just something I threw together."

"Hardly, sir," Franklin responded. "It's magnificent. Is this how you control minds?"

"Of course not, lad. A machine cannot control minds! This merely transmits my will over a larger area. It takes years and years of training to control minds, dear boy."

"So that's how you do it. Thank you, Franklin."

"No worries." Franklin stepped back.

The doctor's face turned as red as Father Christmas's cloak when he realized he had been duped again.

Composing himself, he continued, "No matter. Your interference last night just caused me to move up my plans. I shall have a great gift for London later this morning, and you shan't be able to do anything about it. By the time you find me, there will already be far too many under my control. After that, the Queen. I have no doubt that I will rule all that England rules by sunset tonight. And"–he looked over at Ashe–"I know that takes at least one of you out of the game."

Ashe balled his fists and tried to move past me at his supernatural speed. Fortunately for him, I was just as fast and strong. I put my arm up to hold him back and looked up at him. His eyes were dark and full of rage.

"Hold him back, now. Or this place just might need more of a dusting." Dr. Pilkington ran his finger along the dusty top of the wainscoting.

He, like Fanny, knew what Ashe was, which meant he was at least as powerful as Fanny was. Not good.

"How did you know?" I asked, still trying to stall just a little longer. *Just allow Fanny to finish her spell.*

"I can see only darkness inside him. Plus, if you remember, I controlled him not too long ago. It was actually something I had not tested before, whether or not I could affect the supernatural. Thanks to your little break in, now I know I can. Just think how much more powerful my army will be now with the undead under my control as well as the living. The world will be mine."

"You are the one who is insane," Conrad's mother said.

"Why, Laura. You are looking as lovely as ever," Dr. Pilkington sneered, the tone alone ensured that she knew she looked anything but lovely. The poor woman had obviously been tortured and worse for months. It was amazing that the hell she had endured in that place didn't drive her insane if she had not been before.

"You leave her alone," Conrad put his arm protectively in front of his mother.

"Such a brave boy you have got there, Laura," Dr. Pilkington said. "Such a shame you abandoned him when he needed you most."

Conrad's mum cried out in grief and collapsed on the floor crying. Conrad stooped to her aid, and Dr. Pilkington just laughed. Ashe surged ahead again, but I kept him back.

"See," he said. "I don't need magic or even science to control people. She did exactly what I wanted her to do. Oh. I'm quite good. Indeed. People, even vampires, are so very predictable."

"Do your worst." Fanny stepped out from behind me.

"Oh, I shall, my dear. I certainly shall," he said. "You were quite the looker in your day, were you not, my dear witch? Finished with your little spell are you? You know, when this is all over and I'm the King of England, and thereby most of the world, I shall need a Queen by my side."

Fanny and I both shuddered.

"Or perhaps I shall take a younger wife." His eyes trailed down my body and then back up again, and I felt as if I would vomit. "Or perhaps both, for variety. I will make the laws, after all. You shall both come around, no doubt. Once I control all your minds, you will come around, and what fun we shall have."

Fanny raised her hand as if to cast a spell.

"None of that, my darling." Dr. Pilkington raised the arm with the machine. Without a word or incantation, his movement sent Fanny flying backward into a padded chair. She caught herself from falling over backwards.

"Leave her alone!" I shouted.

"I, actually, shall leave you all alone. Thank you for this little display. I was never going to try to hypnotize any of you again, but this has all been quite...educational. Now I have a good sense of the witch's power, and I know there is a vampire among you. And you, my dear," he said to me. "You are protected by that one's magic from my mind control, but you are more powerful still. The rest, children and the insane."

When he said children, he looked directly at Franklin, trying to cut him for his trick.

It was the momentary distraction we needed. Ashe and I rushed him together, for it was only me who had been holding Ashe back. The two orderlies, instead of pointing their shocking-rods at us, which is what I expected and was prepared for, they both shocked the doctor simultaneously.

The doctor laughed in delight as only a madman can and put his hands up catching us both in our chest.

I first felt a painful shock course through my body, setting every pore on fire, and then...

Blackness.

CHAPTER SEVENTEEN

IN WHICH NICKIE NICK DIES

"She has no heartbeat!" I heard Fanny say, but it sounded so far away, like I was in another room or down a long hallway.

"No! Nickie!" Ashe yelled, and I saw him beneath me, as if I was looking at him from atop a staircase. He was holding someone in his arms. Someone dressed all in black, save for white spats.

It was me! I was somehow looking at myself and everything from above, floating above the room. For there was no staircase or balcony or anything. I floated in midair.

"Do something!" Conrad screamed at Ashe.

His mother sank down into a chair and covered her mouth. She just rocked back and forth, back and forth, saying, "No, no, no, no, no," over and over again.

Franklin held Cassie close to him and Rufus held Edwin. The two youngest were trembling in their silent tears.

"Do something!" Conrad screamed at Ashe again. "Don't just sit there, you freak, do something!" He grabbed Ashe's shoulder and pulled him off me.

"What happened?" Ashe bent down close to my face and put his ear to my chest. "Just a moment ago we were facing the doctor, and now he's gone and Nickie is..."

"He threw you back with some force," Conrad said. "Don't you remember?"

"I remember a sharp pain, then waking up next to Nickie like this. How long was I out?"

"Not even a few seconds," Conrad screamed. "Why are we going through this, vampire? Why aren't you laying there lifeless instead of Nickie?"

"He shocked you." Fanny's tears flowed down her wet, puffy cheeks. "Those rods his men held, they held some kind of electricity. Nicole told me about them when she came to wake me. He seemed to channel the force, perhaps mixing it with magic and–"

"Science," Franklin offered. "That machine on his arm. I bet it can do more than he said."

"If electricity stopped her heart," Fanny said. "Perhaps another jolt would restart it?"

"And where are we going to get electricity from, lady?" Conrad looked at her as if she was some intruder, a stranger. To him she was. Tears ran down his face, too. Poor Conrad. He'd had a really traumatic evening.

"Stand back." Franklin approached my body. Fanny and Ashe moved back, as they clearly didn't know what to do. It didn't even occur to me until now that I could just try to go back into my body, since I was still here after all. Or perhaps this was what death was. Maybe I was a ghost, and that was why I could see all this happening.

Franklin laid my body on its back and put my arms out, stretching away from my body, then he folded them in onto my chest and pushed down. He did the same thing over and over, and the others just looked on, waiting.

Fanny mumbled words of magic or prayer, I couldn't tell which. Conrad's mum stood behind her son with her hands on his shoulders. The younger ones gathered close to Conrad, as he was their protector. And Ashe just looked lost. His face held the grief I felt when I thought he had been dead. I suppose we all had a really traumatic evening.

Then, a strong force began to pull me down from the ceiling and next thing I knew I was coughing. I could feel Ashe's arm around me, holding me close.

"We thought we had lost you, girl." Fanny wiped her rose cheeks dry.

My eyes focused and I looked up at everyone crowded around me. Tear-filled faces changed to smiles when they saw me looking at them.

"Great thinking, Franklin." Conrad patted him on the back. "That seemed to do the trick, all right."

"But of course," Franklin said. "It is The Silvester Method of respiration. Do you never read, Conrad?"

Conrad just laughed and patted him on the back again. The rest joined in, all relieved at my revival. Ashe hugged me tighter until I couldn't breathe.

"Where is Dr. Pilkington?" I choked, and Ashe loosened his grip.

"Escaped," Fanny admitted. "He shocked you and Ashe. Then he and his thugs were gone."

"We have got to stop him," I said. "You all heard what he is going to do."

"How are we going to stop him, Nickie? You heard what he said!" Conrad threw his hands up in exasperation. He'd had enough of all this. He probably just wanted to be back in the dank basement not knowing about any of it. Him and me both.

"That was just to intimidate us, Conrad. We've got to stop him, as we are the only ones who can. He's going to take over England through mass hypnosis. We cannot just let that happen!" I stood up, and I was suddenly feeling strong again. The momentary weakness following my revival and out of body experience passed, and I was ready to take on all of London. If Dr. Pilkington got his way, I might just have to.

"Did you protect everyone against harmful magic, Fanny?" I asked, ready to formulate a plan.

She nodded. "I did, but it was just a temporary field. It shall wear off soon."

"Can you bewitch something that everyone here could carry, like you did for Conrad's compass?" I asked, pulling the compass out of its little pocket in my corset.

"Is that your father's compass?" Mrs. Hannon asked, moving toward me.

"It is, Mum, but I gave it to Nickie for her birthday. She's taken care of us, mum." When you didn't was most certainly implied at the end of that sentence, but it was left unsaid. Mrs. Hannon nodded, knowingly.

"I'm so glad it is in good hands," she said with a kind look towards me. "I had been afraid the police got it, or that horrible man." Her face twisted into rage for a moment, and I knew she spoke about Dr. Pilkington.

"That's a fine idea, Nickie. A fine idea," Fanny answered. "Everyone, give me something of yours and I shall bless it with the same protective magic that I did Nickie's compass. It must be something you keep with you always."

I opened up the compass in my palm. The needle spun around once, and then pointed straight to Ashe. Good to know it worked in that capacity, too. Snapping it shut, not wanting to open that discussion again, I said, "Perfect, Fanny. We will all get through this day yet."

Cassie walked up to Fanny and handed over her doll.

Fanny took the doll and hugged it close to her breast. "I hear this is already a magical doll, ain't that right Cassie?"

Cassie just nodded, never smiling. She always kept the same little pout on her face.

"Can it be anything?" Edwin reached down into his pocket and pulled out a small stone. "I always carry this rock in my pocket. It's for good luck."

"That's just perfect, Edwin," Fanny said smiling. The rest each gave her something of theirs to bless, and Fanny went into the kitchen for some privacy to work.

"All right. Next, how can we stop this madman from taking over London." Each of their faces stared blankly back at me.

"How about we call the police?" Mrs. Hannon finally offered to break the silence. "Is that just too obvious to work?"

"What shall we tell the police, Mrs. Hannon? That a madman is going to hypnotize all of London in a plot to take over the world?" I tried not to sound sarcastic, but I didn't do a very good job of it. She looked rather wounded, and Conrad glared at me. "I'm sorry, Mrs. Hannon. It actually would be a fine idea if he was a regular criminal, but I just don't think we have time right now for that. He is too powerful, and he is going to act quickly. Likely his first target will be the police, to avoid further problems with his plan.

"Ashe," I continued, turning to him. "What did he mean that you would be out of the game until sundown?"

"It is a widely held belief that vampires cannot be out in the daylight, but that's only partially true. We are weaker during the day, but still a good deal stronger than your average man. Direct sunlight will burn our skin, making it blister after prolonged exposure, more that just a few minutes. After about an hour, things get progressively worse until it causes us to combust."

"Direct sunlight? It is winter in London, even in summer there is hardly direct sunlight, so you are still able to work with us?"

"Until the end," he said, looking deeply into my soul.

CHAPTER EIGHTEEN

IN WHICH NICKIE NICK DEVISES A BIG PLAN

*A*she and I stole away into the street below briefly, away from the chattering boys while Fanny was still at work. It was considerably colder outside than in, but one look at Ashe, and I warmed right up. It was just after dawn, but there was no sunlight to speak of. Another grey morning in South London. Perfect.

"I don't know what I would have done." He ran a cold finger down my cold cheek. He stood very close in front of me as I leaned up against the wall in the neighboring alley. "I thought I had lost you."

My heart swelled and I suddenly felt the need to take off my scarf and hat, as I was getting quite warm. He leaned down and touched my lips with his, just for a moment before pulling away and stepping back.

"Is everything all right?" I asked, not liking that he was so far away from me now. I wanted to pull him closer again. Let him cover me and pin me against the wall.

"We cannot," he said.

"We cannot...what?" I asked.

"This." He pointed to himself and then to me and then back to himself. "Us."

"What us, Ashe. We've just only met." I got rather annoyed.

"With this mad doctor trying to take over London and the Queen and probably Parliament, too, while he is at it. How can we think about ourselves at a time like this, not to mention your safety with me?"

"What did you say?"

"I said, I don't trust your safety with me, when you are so close and you smell so good." He made a motion as if he would come back to me, but then stopped himself.

"No. Before that." A plan began to formulate. "You said he would want to take over the Queen and likely Parliament, too."

"Yes."

"But Parliament isn't in session today. It's Christmas Day. How will he get them all in one place, or at least near enough for his mesmerism trick to work?"

"He plans on taking the entire city, Nickie. They're all within the city, aren't they?"

"Indeed they are," I answered. "But he would be much more powerful if he could get the Queen and all of Parliament at once. Then there would be no one left to stop him."

"But like you said, it's Christmas Day. They aren't all in one place."

Just then, I heard the faint chimes of Big Ben across the city. It must have been quite a quiet morning if they could be heard this far away. I counted the chimes. Eight. It was officially morning now, and my parents were likely beside themselves with both me and Fanny gone. Hopefully, they thought the two of us went out for a special Christmas morning treat or something. I didn't waste too much thought on it, though, as there were larger things at stake here. If we failed today, there would be no Christmas for anyone. Not my family or any family. There would be no families anymore, just a million zombies, all working for the mad Dr. Pilkington.

I took Ashe by the hand and pulled him toward me, kissing him again. He didn't pull back, despite his words from before. I drank in his taste and scent. I reveled in the feeling of bliss as he held me close and my lips pressed against his. I studied every sensation, determined to hold on to this feeling for what lie ahead.

He pressed against me and deepened the kiss, brushing his tongue with mine. The ball of excitement that filled my stomach whenever he was near sank a little lower. The next moment, he pulled away, and I was glad he did, for I had not the strength to do so. Although he still remained close, looking into my eyes and I saw forever there.

The December air stung my lips, still wet with his kiss, but there was work to do.

"Follow me," I breathed, barely above a whisper. "We have work to do."

Back upstairs, Fanny was finished with her work in the kitchen and the others were talking amongst themselves.

"The police are coming," Cassie screamed to us when we entered the room.

"She has been saying that for a few minutes now. Where did you two go?" Fanny asked with an accusatory look.

Blushing, I ignored the question and turned to Cassie. "What, Cassie? The police?"

"Yes. My dolly says so. Will you believe me this time?" She stomped her little foot and crossed her arms over her doll.

"Of course, we believe you, Cassie." She hadn't been mistaken yet. Whatever power this little girl had, it was very real. "When are they coming?"

"Soon."

Great. That was specific.

"Dr. Pilkington probably went to the police first, now they're under his control to help him take the rest of the city without resistance," I offered. "Fanny, would you be able to break the spell by sound instead of taste?"

Fanny cocked her head and looked at me quizzically. "You mean like a spoken spell? I suppose. I'd have to do some research."

"Not a spoken spell, no, but by a single sound, like, for example, the chiming of bells? Could you bewitch the bells to break the spell?"

"I like the way you think, girl!" Fanny exclaimed, rising from her seat. Excitement swam in her eyes. She looked more alive and younger than I'd ever seen her, and I realized just how much of herself she had given up to raise me. To train me.

"He'll likely begin near Parliament and the Queen. Once he has them controlled, he doesn't need to control everyone in London, because he controls the power of London. The power of England. And if he controls England, the world is not far behind."

"Of course, but Parliament does not meet today. It's Christmas Day," Fanny said.

"Yes. That's the only part I haven't figured out."

"Well, if he already has the police under his hypnosis spell, perhaps they've alerted the government in some sort of emergency," Frankin suggested.

"It's as possible as anything," I said. "Cassie says the police are coming, so we had better get out while we can." Fanny and Ashe nodded, as I was speaking directly to them. "No doubt they're coming to keep us inside, among other things. We must get out before they get here."

Conrad went to put on his coat.

"No, Conrad." I knew he was not going to like this. "You need to stay here with your mum, and the others. It is up to you to protect them. You are the man here, and we're counting on you to keep everyone safe."

Conrad, rather than protest this time, held his chin up, proud.

His mother looked at him, swelling with pride as well.

"Franklin, can you give me any information about that contraption on Dr. Pilkington's arm? He said that he was somehow using that to manipulate these people."

"It looked steam-driven, judging from the pressure gauge on the shoulder along with the copper tubes running down the side. I'm not sure exactly how it transmits, but however it works it will no longer do so if you release the steam. Break those copper tubes, or even the pressure gauge. That should do it."

"Great, Franklin. Thanks." Turning to my partners in this absurd plan, I continued, "Fanny, Ashe, you both are with me. We must get out of here before the cops come. We will have to stay out of sight, as Dr. Pilkington can see through their eyes now, and he will recognize us."

"How are we to remained unseen?" Fanny asked.

"Fanny the Nanny, get ready to get a little dirty."

CHAPTER NINETEEN

IN WHICH NICKIE NICK
SHOWS OFF HER NEW DRESS

*A*she began to lower Fanny into the sewer, and
I couldn't help but laugh. The sight of a none-
too-small, red-haired Scottish woman coming down
towards me had that affect. It gave me a wave of joy
amidst all the tension over the past few days. Her legs
wiggled beneath her black skirts, swishing her petticoat
back and forth in the most amusing way. Looking up,
I saw Ashe bracing himself with a foot on either side of
the round sewer opening, squatting as he lowered Fanny
down by her outstretched arms. He caught my eye and
smiled, and nearly started laughing himself. When she
was far enough down, I grabbed round her waist and
took her weight down the rest of the way. Her pointy
boots splashed in the foul water beneath.

"Blimey!" she exclaimed, daintily lifting her skirts,
and I laughed anew. My laughter echoing along the
walls of the sewer. Ashe lowered himself in, hanging by
one arm while the other pulled the cover back over the

hole. He dropped to the ground with the grace of a cat. No sound. No splash.

A little more than an hour later, Ashe had navigated us to just behind my house. I exited first, ensuring the sun was still behind a thick layer of clouds, which, of course, it was, (December. London. Of course.) and there was no one in sight. I helped lift Fanny back up with Ashe's help from below. Perhaps it was again the image of Fanny's swinging pantaloon legs beneath her skirt that set me giggling again, knowing that Ashe was getting the same view now, but I forced myself to stay steady, lest I drop the poor woman down on Ashe's head.

"This situation is bad enough here, lassie," she said sternly as she planted her feet on the cobblestones. "I don't need your mockery, as well!" She made as to slick her hair back, but she must have caught a foul smell on her hands for her face twisted in a grimace and she dropped her hand, looking at it with disgust.

Ashe came topside and we all made our way to the house. Fanny led us around to the front door. No use sneaking in and pretending we were there the entire time. We most certainly had already been missed on Christmas morning.

"Let me take care of your parents, love." We mounted the stoop. Fanny took a key from a chain around her neck and opened the front door. "Hello?" she said.

"Where have you been," my father raged as he came marching toward the front door. "Your mother and I have been frantic! This is a fine Christmas gift, young lady. Explain yourself." The rage turned to shock when he saw my outfit. He opened his mouth again to shout some more, but Fanny spoke before he could.

"I'm afraid it is my fault, Mr. Hawthorn," Fanny began, and I saw her wave her hand, like she had done with Lucian. My father's gaze went blank for a moment and then cleared up. "We went out for some hot sweet rolls as a surprise," Fanny put her hands forward as if she was handing him a box of hot bakery, and he took it with a big smile.

"Well, That's quite the surprise, Fanny. Thank you! Greta," he called to my mother in the next room. "Look at what Fanny and Nicole brought for us as a Christmas treat! Piping hot sweet rolls."

My mother came in with a scowl that also turned to a smile with another wave of Fanny's hand. This was all too great. The best Christmas gift ever!

"Thank you, Fanny," my mother said. "My, Nicole, you look quite beautiful! Is that a new dress?"

I looked down at my filthy slaying uniform, covered in sewer water, but I went with it. "It is, Mum. A gift from Fanny for Christmas. Do you like it?" I asked, twirling around.

"My dear, you look simply fetching in it. Lord Godwyn will be so pleased when he visits this afternoon."

"Lord Godwyn," Ashe said from behind me, still outside.

"Yes," my mother continued, looking up and smiling as if she knew him. "Lord Godwyn is going to marry our daughter. Isn't it wonderful?"

"Truly," Ashe growled through clenched teeth.

I turned to him and shook my head, hoping he would know that I most certainly had no intention of marrying Lord Godwyn.

"Miss Hawthorn might have mentioned that to me." His nostrils flared and his eyes bore into me.

"Ashe," I said sweetly. "Why are you still out in the cold."

"It is impolite for a gentleman to enter a lady's home without an express invitation. Impossible, actually." He glared at me.

"Do come in, Ashe," I said.

Fanny looked at me crossly. "I do hope you know what you are doing, lassie."

"Yes, do come in!" my mother echoed, as Ashe stepped over the threshold.

"Now, you and the missus go and begin opening your gifts," Fanny said to my father. "We shall be in presently."

"Splendid idea." My father offered his arm to my mother, who took it, and they left the room together, nearly skipping.

"That was brilliant!" I said to Fanny as we made our way upstairs with Ashe. "Can you do that anytime?"

"Of course, but I shan't be covering for you for just anything, young lady." Fanny gave a stern look at Ashe, who was walking just behind us up the main staircase. She left us at my chamber and before going on to her own said, "Give me must just a minute, and I shall meet you. Just a minute." She was sure to emphasize that we would not be alone together long.

We stepped into my chamber, and I suddenly felt flush. No man other than my father had ever been in my bedchamber.

"Nice room." Ashe looked around at the rosy frills and various shades of pink. He kept his hands folded behind him and didn't step in any further than just inside the door.

I went over to my dressing table, and I was afraid to look at myself. As soon as I saw my reflection, I knew I should not have looked. There were stray hairs coming out the sides from all down the long braid. There was something very dark smudged on my cheek, and I had not felt anything. "Oh my goodness!" I exclaimed, and rushed over to the wash basin. Dipping the cloth in the water there, I desperately tried to get the soot, or whatever that was, off my face. I heard movement behind me, but I didn't take my eyes off my dirty face long enough to see. Then, Ashe's hand covered mine, and at first I thought it was my imagination, for there in the mirror, it was still just me. I turned, and he was standing right behind me.

"No reflection," he offered.

"Lucky you." I bowed my head, hiding.

He lifted my chin with his strong hand and kissed me gently. Just once, so softly.

"You are beautiful, Nickie. A little dirt does not change that."

"Ahem," Fanny said emphatically, coming in through our adjoining doorway.

We parted, rather guiltily, but I knew I now didn't need any blush, for my cheeks were plenty rosy at the moment.

"I have got it!" Fanny held up a large tome.

"What is that?" I knew just about every book in father's library, read most of them myself, but this one I had never seen before.

"It is an ancient spell book," she answered. "If your answer lies anywhere, it is in here."

"Good work, Fanny," I said. "Get Lucian to take us to Westminster. Ashe and I will meet you out front."

Fanny looked at us suspiciously and crossed her arms.

"We are going." I pushed Ashe out ahead of me. "Right now."

CHAPTER TWENTY

IN WHICH NICKIE NICK
MEETS QUEEN VICTORIA

Lucian pulled up in front of the Houses of Parliament. Along the entire route, police lined every street, all wearing the same blank stare as the other zombies. Fanny paged through her large tome, and we all kept our faces hidden in the shadows of the carriage on the way. No one seemed to be following us. After all, there were many carriages out, as it was nearing ten o'clock now. Even on a holiday like today, London was an active city.

"Ashe, get her inside quickly and up to the bells. Carry her if you have to." Fanny gave me a warning look. "You might be recognized as soon as you step out," I reasoned. "You will have to move fast."

"That's why I brought this." She held up a folded parasol.

There was no sun, of course, but a parasol never even garnered a second look, on sunny or cloudy days. It was a matter of fashion.

"Brilliant," I said.

Fanny stepped out first, opening her parasol in the open doorway and covering any sight of their faces with it until both she and Ashe were out. Then, with their backs still to the street, Ashe asked me, "Where are you going?"

"Buckingham Palace," I answered. "That's his main target after all, right?"

"Why is the Queen even here on Christmas?" Fanny asked. "She always spends the holiday in the Isle of Wight. Even before Albert passed on."

"I don't know," I admitted, "but that's what the doctor said."

"Be careful," Ashe said with concern in his eyes. "It could be a trap."

I hadn't thought of that.

In thanks, I reached out and touched his hand.

He squeezed it and then brought it to his lips for a kiss. His intense eyes never left mine, and I hadn't realized I had stopped breathing until Fanny pointedly cleared her throat again.

"You, too. Be careful," I warned, and then added, "Keep her safe, Ashe. I'm counting on you."

"I will." He squeezed my hand one more time, winked at me, and then closed the door.

I truly hoped it was not a trap.

The carriage started back up with a jolt and before long, I was clacking my way over to Buckingham Palace. As we passed Parliament Square, a boy had the morning newspaper and was shouting out the headlines.

"Hear ye! Hear ye! Queen to spend Christmas in London for the first time in thirty years. See her leaving Westminster Abbey after morning service. What better way to celebrate this holy day. Hear ye! Hear ye! Queen to spend Christmas in London!"

"That's how," I said to myself. I had been so busy with my new slayer duties, I had not read the papers or kept up with the news. Parliament would be here in honor of the Queen foregoing her normal trip to the Isle of Wright. "Of course," I repeated, then leaning out the window I shouted to Lucian. "Westminster Abbey, Lucian!"

But I had forgotten about being recognized. One copper saw me and blew his whistle immediately, then another joined in. Before I knew it, five different officers were rushing toward the carriage at once. I leapt out and shouted back at Lucian to get out of there fast. Running much faster than the coppers could, I sprinted toward the Abbey.

The coppers followed, but I quickly out-paced them.

My heels hit the cobblestones with a clack-clack as I raced back down Little George Street. I turned onto Parliament Square and ran right into a copper, knocking him to the ground, but I didn't stop. The fallen officer blew his whistle frantically until the shrill sound mixed with the other half dozen police still blowing their whistles as they caught up. They all faded quickly in the background as I picked up speed. The Abbey was only a few more blocks away.

The coppers were still after me, and I was picking up new ones as I ran past each officer spaced along the street to guard the area for the Queen.

But it was no longer her orders they followed.

Sure enough, the entire front lawn of the Abbey was filled with people. There must be thousands waiting to see the Queen. I stopped, sliding a little on the icy sidewalk, then slipped into the assembly. Once in the crowd of people, I moved through them and hid amongst them, making my way to the front.

But I was too late.

As I neared main walkway, I saw Dr. Pilkington, with a fine coat covering his bizarre arm contraption. He stood in front, just on the far side of the walk leading up to the grande entrance. His draped coat made him look much like a hunchback, with one shoulder so much higher than the other.

Mass let out just as I was reached the front, directly across from the mad doctor. The Queen emerged from the magnificent abbey, and the crowd closed in, trying to get a closer look her walking amongst her people.

Pilkington shrugged his coat off as he bowed to the Queen. She nodded, but then gave him a very strange look as he stretched out his arms.

"No!" I shouted, but the entire place was already his. Not only could I feel the change around me, suddenly everyone was looking at me, pointing at me. And everything was silent.

"Bring her to me." The volume of his voice stretched across the entire, silent courtyard. Hands from all the people surrounding me clamped down on my shoulders, my arms, my hair. Groping, clawing hands. I struggled and fought, kicking the people away from me, but there were too many. They just kept coming at me. They shuffled me up to the walkway and spat me out onto the ground,

There I stood before the Queen herself.

I curtsied, even though I was not wearing a skirt and was covered in dirt and likely sewage, because that was what one does in the presence of royalty. But Queen Victoria had the same blank stare as everyone else in the courtyard.

Please, Fanny, I thought. *Please let this work.*

The Queen looked at me with her stern face, for even the blank stare in her eyes didn't make her any less intimidating. This woman ruled most of the known world, and here she was before me. And she was tiny! She was considerably shorter than I, at least an entire head shorter. She had a round face and was covered in very fine jewels. Her dark dress was accented with ivory lace along the collar, and she wore a matching veil.

"Your Majesty." Dr. Pilkington bowed to her as well. What was he playing at? He controlled them all. "May I present my fiancee?" He held his hand out for me, as if I would actually take it. "Introduce yourself to the Queen, my dear."

"I'm not your fiancee, you sick man."

"What a lovely girl, my dear doctor," Queen Victoria said. "You have my blessing to wed."

"Of course we do." Dr. Pilkington looked over at me with love in his eyes. "See, my dear, I told you that you couldn't stop me. In fact, I must thank you. Without your interference yesterday, this all would have taken so much longer. Waiting another week, I wouldn't have had such immediate access to Her Majesty, and with all of Parliament here as well. Yes, I truly owe you a debt of gratitude, dear lady." He grabbed my hand and kissed it before I could yank it away in disgust.

Just then, the Cambridge Chimes rang out, and hope filled my chest.

Please, Fanny, I thought again, for I was truly out of ideas. I closed my eyes and tried to forget that revolting madman was holding my hand. The sound of the bells I held so dear filled my ears. Through my closed eyes, I imagined Ashe before me. Remembering how it felt to kiss him and praying that I would kiss him again.

As the main chimes began to mark the tenth hour of the day, the crowd around me began to chatter amongst themselves. I opened my eyes to see Queen Victoria set her jaw and give a more stern look than ever.

"I beg your pardon" was all she said as she marched by me with her train of people.

I looked up at Dr. Pilkington, and he was stunned into silence. Taking the opportunity, I spun around and with a back kick that activated my stake-heel, smashed the pressure gauge on his shoulder. Steam squealed upward and people around him began to put rather a lot of distance between him and them. He and I were now alone in a ring of people, so, while I had him there, I made something very clear. "I would never marry you, with or without a royal blessing."

Then with a palm strike, I took out the copper tubing running down the side. More steam expelled, and I knew he would not be trying this again anytime soon. His contraption was in shambles.

"But how?" he asked, broken.

Big Ben sang its tenth chime, and I smiled.

His face became a contortion of rage and he spat, "The witch."

CHAPTER TWENTY-ONE

IN WHICH NICKIE NICK
GETS CAUGHT UP IN SOME COGS

D r. Pilkington caught me off guard. Foolish girl. I had thought he was defeated, but fire anew raged in his eyes. He reached out and ripped the pocket compass off my corset. Throwing up his other hand, he mumbled something I didn't understand. After the initial blow hit my chest and knocked the breath from me, I flew backwards into the crowd, landing on top of several confused people.

When I looked up, he was already gone. The people around me complained and chastised me, as if I had any choice in the matter. I staggered to my feet and gave my apologies before running towards the great clock tower.

He was going after Fanny.

People out on this lovely Christmas morning stopped in shock as I ran past them, rounding onto Parliament Square. The Houses were veiled in a blue-grey haze, as it began to snow rather heavily and the temperature seemed to drop another ten degrees. Only the gaslamps along the street and the glow from the great clock face cut through the misty fog. As I ran, I left behind footprints in the thin layer of fresh snow that quickly covered the ground.

As I turned the last corner onto Bridge Street, I saw Dr. Pilkington disappear behind the marble gates surrounding The Houses. I scaled the marble wall, but he was already entering the bottom of the clock tower.

He saw me approaching, and he held up Conrad's pocket compass, taunting me.

I picked up speed and turned into the stone foyer. That madman would get what was coming to him.

The doctor was already behind the interior door. The bottom half was heavy wood, and the top half contained three panes of glass, each column was protected by a long wrought iron frame extending up the length of the glass and topped with a fleur de lis. As I reached for the door handle, the doctor flicked his fingers at me and propelled me into the opposite stone wall.

I really missed that compass.

From the ground, I looked up at the door. Dr. Pilkington waved his hand over the door handle. He caught my eye and smirked before turning away and disappearing inside.

The one door became two doors and then back to one. Stars filled my peripheral vision as I tried to get up, and then fell right back down. The lump on the back of my head from where it hit the stone yelled at me. Finally, I acquired my balance and moved toward the door.

The handle was still quite warm. He must have melted the lock with magic.

It wouldn't budge, even when I jiggled it with my strength. Then I kicked it. Again and again, to no avail.

His spell must have strengthened the door as well. It was the only explanation.

The iron bars prevented me from being able to put my elbow through one of the windows, but not my fist. My hands were gloved, so the damage would be minimal. I threw a punch through the bottom of the glass right above the door handle. Large shards fell. And, even though I pulled back the punch as I had been taught, some of the falling shards cut into my coat and sliced my arm. Superficial, though. No real damage. After the glass had cleared, I reached in, but then realized how thoughtless that had been. It was locked with magic, so I couldn't open it from the inside either. I frantically looked around for another entrance.

Stepping back out onto the grounds, I looked up at the tower. From this vantage point, the large wreath blocked the clock face from view.

"Could scale the side, I suppose."

A man dressed in his Sunday's best led his wife in a rather large circle around me: the mad, filthy, bleeding girl speaking to herself. I pulled the goggles over my eyes, reminding myself of the benefit of not being recognized.

Scaling the side was, of course, preposterous. I headed back inside, determined to get through that door, as it would be faster than finding another entrance into The Houses and then having to navigate my way to the clock tower from within.

Standing very still, I did as Fanny had taught me. I took a fighting stance directly in front of the door and concentrated on the energy coming from the earth. Each time thoughts of what Dr. Pilkington might be doing to Ashe and Fanny came in, I pushed them out of my head and focused on the earth until I felt that tingling sensation again. Once I found it, I honed all my attention in on drawing up that energy into my body, imagining the earth's energy surrounding and filling me with power. I opened my eyes, concentrated on the area around the door handle, and kicked.

It splintered.

I kicked again and again, and the door gave way a little more each time. The last kick, I spun around putting the full force of my strength and determination into kicking through the door, and that time, it gave way. I rushed inside only to find another door exactly like the first, only this one had a brass sign on it that read "Clock Tower."

My heart sunk.

In an act of pure optimism, I tried the handle. Locked and still warm from the magic.

This time, I had no doubt that I could get through. My increasing anger mixed with my power enabled me to kick through this door in only three tries. I shot toward the marble staircase and began ascending it without hesitation, taking the steps two and three at a time.

About halfway up, I saw Dr. Pilkington look over the wrought iron railing. Thankfully he was old and out of shape, so he moved slowly.

I was none of those things.

"You just don't give up, do you, girl?" he shouted down to me.

He thrust his hand over the railing towards me, but I had learned my lesson. Twice. Throwing myself against the opposite railing, I averted the blow then continued my ascent. I caught up with him and dove at his feet, tackling him into a large room with a series of huge, black, silver, and brass gears that stretched across a metal platform situated in the center of the room. Conrad's compass flew from his hand and slid across the floor. Launching off of the doctor, I grappled for the sliding compass, but before I could reach it, I felt another great blow. This one threw me on top of the turning gears. The continuously rotating large cylindrical gear along the edge rolled me over onto the smaller central cogs. I found my footing on one of their axles and tried to get up off them, but I was stuck. The corner of my coat had gotten caught in between two of the turning gears, and it was holding me back.

The doctor laughed and dangled the compass, provoking me again, before he left the room and started up to the next level.

"Fanny," I called out over the clatter of the turning gears. "Ashe! The doctor is coming for you!" I hoped he could hear me with his vampire hearing, but the din of the machinery drowned out my voice. The gear turned another minute and pulled my coat further in.

"Ashe!" I shouted again. Pulling my coat off, I jumped out of the turning gears and dashed upstairs after the doctor. I emerged in the belfry with the five great bells hanging from the rafters. The largest, Big Ben itself, dangled from the center. Surrounding it were the four smaller bells.

Fanny lay collapsed on the floor near the Gothic windows that opened to the outside December air.

"Fanny!" I shouted to her, but she didn't move.

The doctor threw a spell at Ashe, but it didn't affect him, for he still had Fanny's amulet on him. Ashe punched Dr. Pilkington square in the jaw, propelling the madman across the floor.

CHAPTER TWENTY-ONE

"Ashe!" I yelled to him. He turned and flew to my side.

"Are you all right?" he asked, then saw the blood on my arm. "You're hurt."

"I'm fine, Ashe. Fanny?"

"She passed out after the spell," he said. "It must have taken a lot out of her. She's still breathing, though."

"Look out!" I shouted when I saw the doctor stumble towards us.

He threw another spell, but Ashe stepped protectively in front of me.

"Thanks. He's got my compass. I have to get it back, for more than just its magical properties."

The doctor still advanced and tried to throw another spell, but Ashe stepped forward and whacked the doctor with a roundhouse kick, splattering blood along the bottom of Big Ben. The doctor landed near Fanny and the exterior windows, but he got back up on his feet a moment later, faltering but once.

"He just won't stay down," Ashe interjected.

"Not so old and out of shape after all," I mumbled to myself.

"It's his power, Nick. That's what's holding him together. The magic."

The doctor spit blood onto the floor. The front of his coat was soaked with his own blood, but he didn't withdraw. He would not admit defeat. Instead, he held up my compass again, goading me to come after it.

"You're out matched, doctor," I stated calmly, careful to stay behind Ashe as we moved forward together. "Give me the compass, and we'll all get out of here. Together."

"Never, you spoiled brat." His verbal jab was nothing more than an annoyance. "You may think you have defeated me, young lady, but there's fight in me yet. You may have crippled my plans, but machinery can be rebuilt. Plans can be reformed." He darted toward the open window and ran out to the stone balcony. The cold wind whipped through his thinning, grey hair, making it stand on end in a rather comical way. He clutched my compass by the chain in his closed fist and dangled it over the side.

"No!" I lunged towards him, coming out from behind Ashe. In that moment, he sent a magical blast at me so hard that I was thrown back against Big Ben, my skull acting as the chiming hammer. The bell spoke softly, a dull ring that echoed the loud ringing in my ears.

I slid off the great bell back onto my feet. Liquid trickled down the back of my neck. More blood. My knees gave out and I fell to the floor. All I heard was the doctor's maniacal laughter and Ashe's voice.

"Nickie!" Ashe called.

My vision blurred, and I blinked hard trying to regain focus. Two hazy figures danced, silhouetted against the light of day behind them. I couldn't tell which was which, but it seemed like an even fight. The doctor must have cast a spell on himself to increase his own strength, since his magic was useless against Ashe. I slowly emerged from the fog that last blow had caused, and I staggered towards the two engaged figures. Just before I reached them, Dr. Pilkington held up Ashe with both arms stretched over his head and tossed Ashe over the side of the railing.

"No!" I screamed, leaping toward the falling figure, but I was too late again. Dr. Pilkington held out a stiff arm that caught me across the shoulders and threw me back. I tasted blood and coughed, retching red onto the stone balcony.

"Now, you bothersome girl, it is your turn," he snarled as he stepped towards me. The floor moved away from me, and it felt as if I was floating or being held up by an invisible chain. My feet dangled several feet above the stone, and I could see all of London laid out before me. The cold stung my face, but the fallen snow-flakes melting on my skin soothed my many cuts. Tears burned my eyes.

Ashe was gone. Perhaps a vampire could survive that fall, but I would not.

After the doctor was finished with me, he would turn to Fanny. In the end, I was not able to protect any of them. Some Protector I was. I didn't deserve that birthright, and this mess proved it.

The doctor looked up at me, his outstretched arm holding me in place, hovering just over head. He stood there gloating up at me and laughing wildly, knowing he had beat me.

I had not been strong enough to beat him, and now this madman would be back out in London to ruin more lives.

Then the doctor's arm snapped down stiffly to his side, and the stone floor rushed back at me. My body slapped against the stone, causing me to spit up more blood. Darkness threatened to consume me, but then a strong hand touched my bruised body.

"You will be all right, my dove."

"Fanny?"

She helped me to my feet, and I collapsed against her. She held me close to her and kissed my forehead then wiped the blood and tears from my face. She just held me and rocked me gently, like she had done when she sang me lullabies at bedtime when I was a girl.

"It's all right now, my dove. Everything will be all right."

Dr. Pilkington stood stiffly in the same place as before. His face frozen in an expression of surprise, a comical, psychotic statue.

"No, it will not be all right, Fanny," I breathed and pushed away from her. My vision cleared and the reality came flooding back. "This madman killed Ashe." I rushed at the doctor statue and began beating his chest with my fists. "You killed Ashe, you monster! You killed Ashe!"

"You cannot get rid of me that easily, pet."

His voice came from over the side of the building.

The cold London air filled my lungs and hope swelled my heart at the sound of his voice.

"Ashe?"

I rushed to the stone railing and looked over the side. There, hanging from the minute hand, still pointing to the number ten, was Ashe.

"Ashe!" I called. "But how–"

"The wreath, love," he called back. "Happy Christmas." He smiled up at me.

"Happy Christmas, Ashe! Happy Christmas!" I shouted down to him, jumping up and down in my excitement.

Fanny looked over the side next to me. "Luck o' the devil." She shook her head.

"Give us a hand," Ashe said. "Will you, love?"

I leaned over the railing, a little too enthusiastically. It was a very good thing Fanny was there to grab me, or I would have joined Ashe hanging from the clock tower. This was certainly a Christmas Day I would not soon forget.

Ashe balanced near the tip of the minute hand and reached up to me.

"I cannot reach you, Ashe. Wait, and I will find some rope."

"No," he shouted. "I can get closer."

"Don't be foolish, Ashe. I'll get a rope." But before I even moved away from the balcony, Ashe sprang up and grabbed onto the bottom shelf.

"Hold me," I commanded Fanny a second before I leaned far over the balcony, my feet leaving the floor. With a sign of relief, I felt Fanny's hands clasp my ankles just as Ashe reached up and grabbed my wrist. With all my strength, I pulled Ashe up high enough for him to grab the top railing.

After he climbed over the safety railing, he helped Fanny pull me back up. If there was ever a time I was happy I was not wearing skirts, this was it. Although I was quite freezing without my coat, it was probably very good that I didn't have it on during that rescue operation. All that flowiness would have just been in the way.

When my feet were once again firmly on the ground, I swooned. The loss of blood mixed with the head injury and being so recently upside down took its toll. I regained consciousness a moment later in Ashe's arms, exactly where I wanted to be.

CHAPTER TWENTY-TWO

IN WHICH NICKIE NICK
GETS A SPECIAL GIFT

"What shall we do with him?" I asked Fanny, indicating the frozen doctor. "Can we just push him over the side?"

"Nicole Hawthorn!" Fanny scolded.

"I wasn't serious, Fanny. That would be wrong, although rather justified. Still, wrong," I clarified as Fanny looked crossly at me. "Please, Fanny, I wasn't serious."

"Still, you do have a point. We cannot just let him go, nor can we leave him like this."

"He belongs locked away," Ashe offered. "In that hell place he used to run. If anyone deserves a living hell, it is this deranged man."

"Indeed," Fanny agreed.

"But with his powers, what prison could hold him?" I mumbled through my chattering teeth. It was getting colder by the moment, and the snow had not let up. Not even a little bit.

Ashe took his coat off and placed it around my shivering shoulders.

"Thank you, good sir." I smiled up at him, and his returning smile warmed me right up.

"Precisely!" Fanny exclaimed.

Ashe and I exchanged a confused look.

"No prison could hold him, but his own. He must be the prison," Fanny suggested.

"But how?"

"Leave that to me," she said. "Where is your coat, dear girl?"

"Um. Caught in the cogs below."

"Well, you and Ashe go see if you can free it. That cost a pretty penny, it did." Fanny's eyes twinkled.

I hesitated, wondering what she was up to, but she started shooing me and Ashe back into the belfry.

"Just trust me."

We stood there beneath the five great bells, and they began to chime, marking the quarter hour. All that had taken place in a short fifteen minutes, likely the longest quarter hour of my life. As the bells sang around us, Ashe took a moment to kiss me. Softly. His hand cupped the side of my face as he deepened the kiss. His tongue swirled with mine, and I was completely under his control. Again. This moment made the chimes of Big Ben even more special to me than before. If only this moment would freeze in time and I could feel this complete and content always.

"Hem-hem," Fanny interrupted. The bells had stopped ringing, and she stood in the window opening, tapping her pointed toed ankle boots.

"Ooops." I pulled away from Ashe.

The doctor stumbled in from behind her, and I crouched in a fighting stance, ready for whatever he threw at me. Ashe stepped in front of me, protectively.

"Toodle-loo." The doctor swung Conrad's compass from its chain in front of his face. He was dazed, and he stumbled a bit as he walked. "Toodle-loo. Teedle-lee."

"He's cracked," Ashe said.

"And this is news?" Fanny responded.

"What did you do, Fanny?" I walked straight up to the doctor and took my compass out of his hand. He bowed low to me, then walked up to the great bell and banged his head repeatedly on the side of it. A low "dong" rang out with each thud his head made against the bell's side.

"Nothing really," she admitted. "He was quite insane already, as you both well know. I just helped a little."

"Fanny!"

"It was just a forgetting spell, really. I just wanted him to forget who he was and that he had any magical powers. Turns out, the magic was the only thing keeping his mind even a little sane and together. Go figure."

Ashe took me by the hand and descended down the stairs to the lower level. My coat, it seemed, had gone through an entire rotation of the cogs. It now lay in a heap of black oilcloth beneath all the gears. Ashe climbed in and retrieved it for me.

"A little worse for wear." Fanny inspected the damage. It now was imprinted with the shape of the gears. "But nothing Janice cannot fix. Put it back on, my dear. It is rather cold outside, and we have to get you home or all the magic I have will not save you from your parents."

"And the doctor?" I asked.

"I shall hail a policeman down below and tell him about this particular bat in the belfry."

Once back home, safe in my room, I was horrified when I looked in the mirror. What a mess. Blood matted my hair and stained my face. Grabbing the washcloth, I started scrubbing.

Lord Godwyn would be arriving soon, and I definitely couldn't miss that, as much as I wanted to. Mother would never forgive me.

"He just arrived." Fanny rushed into my room and closed the door tight behind her.

"How am I to face him or my parents like this?" I indicated the blood with a wild waving of my hand. Everywhere.

"We shall just clean you up, my dear. Give us your face."

I allowed Fanny to scrub away the blood.

"Does it hurt much?" she asked.

"Not at all actually. They all seem to have healed already. I guess quick healing is one of the great benefits of being The Protector?"

"Indeed," Fanny said as she grabbed a brush. "And, good. Because this will hurt." She forcefully tried to pull the brush through my blood-tangled hair.

"Ow!" I complained. "Do I even have to meet His Most Annoying? I'd rather take a nap. Actually, I'd rather fight the mad psychiatrist again. I'd rather do just about anything than meet with that great fop."

"Now, Nickie," she chided. "It is only for a few hours." She yanked the brush through my dark curls.

"Ow!"

"Perhaps a hat," she offered. "Get those clothes off, love, and get on your proper ones."

I shed the bloody and torn Protector outfit and got into a clean camisole and pair of pantelettes, keeping only the compass and Fanny's necklace close.

Fanny cinched the corset and had me step into a lovely red day dress. Perfect for Christmas Day.

The naughty thought of how I could be a delicious present that Ashe could unwrap next to the fire beneath the holiday tree crossed my mind. They were certainly not proper thoughts for a sweet debutante like me, but it was a nice, brief daydream

Fanny swept up my hair, carefully covering the matted blood until we had a chance to wash it later that day. When she had worked her magic, and not even actual magic this time, no one could tell I had just been in the fight of my life.

A rush of déjà vu flashed through my mind as I began to descend the stairs, just as I had done a short three nights ago when this all started. I made my way into the library, where my parents sat entertaining our guest, Lord Godwyn.

"Ah. Finally," my mother hissed. "How rude of you to keep our guest waiting, Nicole."

"Indeed, Mother. It was rather rude of me." Time to play my other part, at least for awhile. "Please do forgive me, Lord Godwyn."

Reginald stood and reached for my hand to kiss. "You were worth the wait, Miss Hawthorn. A vision of loveliness."

"Oh my! Such a charmer, this one," my mother cooed. "Nicole, you are a lucky girl."

After a quick curtsey to Reginald, I took a seat next to my mother.

"You do look quite lovely this afternoon, Nicole," my father said. "Would you care for a cup of tea?"

"I would love one, Father. Thank you."

Father nodded to our butler waiting off to the side.

Wilfred chanced a wink at me as he handed me a hot cup of tea.

"Thank you, Wilfred," I said. "Do I see an apple tart on the tea cart?"

"Yes, mum," he responded.

"Do you really think you need another apple tart, my dear? You will ruin your supper," my mother injected. "Lord Godwyn has agreed to stay for supper tonight, Nicole. Isn't that delightful?"

"Quite." That was what I said, but what I thought was *You mean I have to endure the rest of the day and evening with His Most Annoying One? This has gotten out of hand.*

Only I could make this stop because mother was not going to let up, so at that moment, I began devising a plan. We went through the rest of tea and exchanged gifts. Mother had bought him those posh gloves from me, but he looked down his nose at them as a paltry gift. Although he thanked me properly, I could see his discernment behind the false smile.

His gift to me was a triple-strand pearl choker that had a beautiful cameo dangling from its center. It truly was a lovely gift and a gorgeous necklace, but I still wanted to smack him when he said that I could now throw out the odious one I had worn the night of my birthday.

That was the last straw.

"Lord Godwyn, would you care to take a turn around the grounds before supper?" I used my most proper and charming debutante voice.

Mother gave father a very approving look, which he returned in kind.

"I would be delighted, Miss Hawthorn," Reginald replied. He took my gloved hand and led me to the foyer.

After donning our coats, I took his arm, as was proper, and we went outside. Alone. Which only went to prove just how much mother wanted me to marry him. Otherwise, we would be chaperoned.

We walked along quietly for a few moments, which rather surprised me, as His Most Annoying was usually prattling along about something or another. As we reached the bench beneath the vine-covered arbor, he turned to me and came in for a kiss. He took me by such complete surprise, that I didn't have time to react. It was sloppy and very wet, and I most certainly didn't kiss back. He seemed to want to inhale my entire face.

At that moment, the sun appeared, peeking through the otherwise grey skies. A complete anomaly in London, especially on Christmas Day.

Something moved quickly into the shadows across the street, but by the time I looked, there was nothing there.

"You see, my dear Nicole. God smiles on us." Reginald swooped down to kiss me again.

I stopped him fully this time by pushing him away, and none too lightly.

"Now see here, Miss Hawthorn," Reginald exhaled with his foul breath. He grabbed me tightly around the waist and tried to force me to him. "If you are to be my wife, there are certain wifely duties to which you must submit, and often. As often as I wish."

His offensive mouth clasped down over mine again. I brought my knee up hard between his legs and it found its mark, for His Most Annoying howled.

"I beg your pardon, Mr. Godwyn."

Reginald doubled over, holding his crotch and sat back onto the bench.

"That's Lord Godwyn to you, my sweet. You will be quite fun to tame. Yes, indeed. Quite fun." His lascivious grin made my stomach turn, and not in a good way. This repugnant man just made my Ashe shine all the brighter.

"How completely revolting. You are not, nor will you ever be, my lord. And most certainly not my husband. I saw you last night, Reginald, you great fop. I saw you with those two strumpets. I know what you are, and you disgust me. This is how it will go." I settled myself next to him on the bench and gave him his instructions.

"You will go back inside and have a lovely dinner with my family. You will act as if everything is fine between us, like I'm always forced to do. Then when dinner is over, you will politely take your leave and then never come back here again. *Never, ever again.* Is that understood?"

"Are you daft, girl? Just who do you think you are addressing?" His ruddy face became even redder as his anger mounted.

"I'm addressing His Most Annoying One, the great fop, Lord Reginald Godwyn. I don't wish to marry you, sir. I don't even wish to ever see you again. You will do as I request, Reginald, or you will most certainly see what I'm capable of, sir."

The sun went back behind the clouds, and I was glad. The sun hurt my eyes anyway. I did love London's grey skies. The sun could stay behind them forever, as far as I was concerned.

Reginald stood up, straightened his waistcoat, and strode back towards the house.

I remained on the bench for another moment and thought of my Ashe. After taking the compass out of my bodice, I looked at the inscription "To Find Your Way Back To Me," remembering how it pointed straight to my love. I opened it. It spun around once and then pointed to me. I spun around, looking across the street behind me, but there was no one there.

Perhaps he would visit me this evening, after the sun went down.

Surprisingly, Lord Godwyn did exactly as I had asked. He likely didn't know how to deal with a strong woman, so he decided that he would rather not. Fine by me.

Dinner was pleasant, then he left. I knew I would never see him again, and mother would just have to find a way to deal with her disappointment. After all, it would seem like his decision.

I happily ascended the staircase, my soft bed calling me after a most trying day. My thoughts went to Ashe. I wondered what he was doing this fine night, and I hoped that I would see him again tomorrow. He was likely as exhausted as I was tonight.

Fanny sat waiting in my chamber when I entered.

"I think I got rid of His Most Annoying, and for good." I unpinned my hair, letting it fall over my shoulders.

"Yes. I saw your little show in the garden," she said. "Quite a good show, it was."

"Yes. Quite. It was rather fun, even." I laughed when I thought about Lord Godwyn doubled over in pain and that stupid look on his face when I told him how it would be. Yes. It turned out to be a very good Christmas after all.

"This came for you while you were at dinner." Fanny held out a single red rose, a small package, and a note.

My heart leapt. "Ashe?"

"Who else, my lamb?"

I took the gifts from Fanny and plopped down on my bed, excited to open them. I placed the rose on my pillow after smelling its sweet scent, hoping it would enable me to dream of my love all night. Then I unwrapped the small box. Inside was a skeleton key. A small, tarnished skeleton key, just like the ones Ashe wore dangling on that ring from his waistcoat.

"Curious." I opened the envelope next. Here is what the letter said:

My Dearest Nicole,

I cannot express how the last few days have changed me. Meeting you was like bathing in sunlight again. I fancied that I actually felt my heart beat again when our lips met.

The key is to my heart, for it is yours. Only yours. Always yours.

Yet, when I saw you in the sunlight today with your beau, I knew that's where you belonged. In the sunlight, not in the darkness with me. My heart is yours, my love, but you must save your heart for someone who can dance with you in the sunlight.

Don't look for me, for you will not find me. The boys are fine. I checked on them, and I will continue to do my work and keep a watch over you and the boys as well, but I will do so from a distance.

Thank you, my love, for reminding me what is was like to feel.

Always,

      Ashe

The words on the page blurred through my tears. I tossed the letter aside and ran into Fanny's arms. Her smile faded as she caught my falling figure.

"What is it, my lamb? What did the letter say?"

"He's gone, Fanny. Ashe is gone." I clasped the key tightly in my hand until the sharp corner cut into my flesh.

"Gone?" Fanny asked.

"Yes. Gone, but he's a fool, Fanny." I dried my tears and stood up. Opening my palm, I looked at the key spotted with my blood. The key to his heart. I would keep it next to my heart along with Fanny's amulet.

After stringing the key through the chain and tucking it down inside my camisole, I vowed that I would find him. I would show him that I belonged in the darkness, with him.

OTHER BLUE MOOSE PRESS TITLES

Rowan of the Wood
Winner of the 2009 Indie Excellence Award
978-0-9819949-2-5 $12.95 trade paperback
After a millennium of imprisonment in his magic wand, an
ancient wizard possesses the young boy who released him. When
danger is nigh, he emerges from the frightened child to set things
right. Both he and the boy try to grasp what has happened to them
only to discover a deeper problem. Somehow the wizard's bride
from the ancient past has survived and become something evil.
http://www.rowanofthewood.com

Witch on the Water
Rowan of the Wood: Book Two
978-0-9819949-2-5 $12.95 trade paperback
Cullen thought he had enough trouble surviving school, dealing
with his miserable home life, and being possessed by Rowan, a
1400-year-old wizard. But when Rowan's wife, the sadistic vampire Fiana, comes back seeking revenge, Cullen and his band of
misfits must do what they can to stop her. This time Cullen's
favorite teacher is Fiana's first target.

Fire of the Fey
Rowan of the Wood: Book Three
978-0-9819949-6-3 $12,95 trade paperback
Adventures continue for Cullen Knight and his band of misfits in
this third installment of the Rowan of the Wood fantasy series.
Still possessed by the wizard Rowan, Cullen settles into his new
home with his fire elemental sister, Aidan, and their fey uncle,
Moody Marlin. But all is not well. A series of fires raging through
the redwoods puts Aidan in the hot seat, as the group looks to her
for an explanation.

Power of the Zephyr
Rowan of the Wood: Book Four
978-1-936960-94-1 $12.95 trade paperback
Power of the Zephyr continues the Rowan of the Wood fantasy
series with further adventure and magical mayhem. The Freak
Squad, as Trudy takes to calling them, confront Fiana in the des-
ert of Northern Nevada. She has developed a cult of mesmerized
zombies in an intricate plot to capture Rowan and his wand for
herself, once and for all.

Other by O. M. Grey

Avalon Revisited
978-0-9819949-5-6 $12.95 trade paperback
Arthur Tudor has made his existence as a vampire bearable for over
three hundred years by immersing himself in blood and debauch-
ery. Aboard an airship gala, he meets Avalon, an aspiring vampire
slayer who sparks fire into Arthur's shriveled heart. Together they
try to solve the mystery of several horrendous murders on the dark
streets of London. Cultures clash and pressures rise in this sexy
Steampunk Romance.
http://omgrey.wordpress.com

Re-released, January 2013 by Riverdale Ave Books. Check
Amazon for this title in paperback and for the Kindle as well as
the publisher's website: http://riverdaleavebooks.com

The Zombies of Mesmer
978-1-936960-92-7 $12.95 trade paperback
Gothic YA paranormal romance novel
Follow Nicole Knickerbocker Hawthorn (Nickie Nick) as she dis-
covers her destiny as The Protector, a powerful vampire hunter.
Ashe, a dark and mysterious stranger, helps Nickie and her friends
solve the mystery behind several bizarre disappearances. Suitable
for teens, enjoyed by adults.

COMING SUMMER 2013, a second installment in the Nickie
Nick Vampire Hunter series!

Keep watch on http://omgrey.wordpress.com

Caught in the Cogs: An Eclectic Collection
978-1-936960-90-3 $12.95 trade paperback
In the midst of war, a beautiful young officer finds love aboard an
airship...A woman steals away to fulfill her desire with a phantom
lover...A group of thieves seek out a town of women to satisfy their
lustful urges, but these ladies have an agenda of their own...

PLUS nine more short stories, angsty love poetry, and twenty-six
relationship essays considering topics such as alternative lifestyles,
deepening intimacy, opening communication, abusive relation-
ships, and how to end a relationship with respect.

MORE BLUE MOOSE PRESS AUTHORS

Prelude to a Change of Mind
Hidden Lands of Nod: Book One
978-0-9827426-0-0 $9.95 trade paperback
Meg Christmas is found sick unto death in a remote mountain
camp. Beings out of legend arrive to save her, emerging from an
alternate realm where they live in exile. A quiet, intimate adventure, *Prelude to a Change of Mind* boasts dire peril and brave feats,
but also lots of tea with Ekaterina Rigidstick, poems by Jack
Plenty, and talks with both about the nature of reality and condi-
tions of being.

Entranscing
Hidden Lands of Nod: Book Two
978-0-9827426-2-4 $9.95 trade paperback
The second book in *The Hidden Lands of Nod* revisits Meg and her
friends from the exile realms of the Dvarsh–the metamathemage,
Ekaterina Rigidstick, and her cousin, the part-human poet,
Jackanapes Plenty–in a vastly different reality twenty years on.
This fast-moving follow-on to *Prelude to a Change of Mind* picks
up and enlarges the tale of Meg, the Dvarsh, the Thrm, and their
collective struggle to save both love and the planet.
http://www.robertstikmanz.com

Fiends: Volume One
978-1-936960-00-2 $35.00 Limited Edition Hardback
978-1-936960-01-9 $12.95 trade paperback
Including Canvas, Tattoo, and Closet Treats, Fiends: Vol 1 is a collection of horror stories by Paul E. Cooley. As a special treat, the
author gives his reader a glimpse into the FiendMaster's Scrapbook.

THANK YOU SO MUCH FOR READING.

I HOPE YOU ENJOYED
THE ADVENTURES OF NICKIE NICK.

PLEASE CONSIDER WRITING A
REVIEW ON AMAZON.COM AND
GOODREADS. JUST A FEW SENTENCES
IS SO VERY APPRECIATED.

PLEASE SHARE IT ON YOUR
NETWORKS & RECOMMEND IT TO
YOUR FRIENDS!

PEACE.

ABOUT THE AUTHOR

Nestled in the mountains of Northern California, Olivia M. Grey lives in the cobwebbed corners of her mind writing paranormal romance with a Steampunk twist. She dreams of the dark streets of London and the decadent deeds that occur after sunset. As an author of Steamy Steampunk, as well as a poet, blogger, podcaster, and speaker, Olivia focuses both her poetry and prose on alternative relationship lifestyles and deliciously dark matters of the heart and soul. Her work has been published in various anthologies and magazines like Stories in the Ether, Steampunk Adventures, SNM Horror Magazine and How The West Was Wicked.

Her premiere Steampunk BDSM erotica novel, Avalon Revisited, is an Amazon.com Gothic Romance bestseller. She also currently has two other titles available: The Zombies of Mesmer, a YA Steampunk Romance, Caught in the Cogs: An Eclectic Collection of short stories, love poetry, and relationship essays.

Ms. Grey is represented by the fabulous Louise Fury of the L. Perkins Agency.

Visit her online at http://omgrey.wordpress.com
On Twitter: @omgrey
On Facebook: http://facebook.com/OMGREY